Bright's Pas

Bright's Passage

A Novel

Josh Ritter

The Dial Press
New York

Published in the United States by The Dial Press, an imprint of The Random House Publishing Group, a division of Random House, Inc., New York.

DIAL PRESS is a registered trademark of Random House, Inc., and the colophon is a trademark of Random House, Inc.

LIBRARY OF CONGRESS CATALOGING-IN-PUBLICATION DATA
Ritter, Josh.
Bright's passage: a novel/Josh Ritter.
p. cm.
ISBN 978-1-4000-6950-7
eBook ISBN 978-0-6796-0425-9
1. World War, 1914–1918—Veterans—West Virginia—Fiction.
2. Appalachian Region—Social life and customs—Fiction. I. Title.
PS3618.I785B75 2011
813'.6—dc22   2010035308

Printed in the United States of America on acid-free paper

www.dialpress.com

4 6 8 9 7 5

FIRST EDITION

Book design by Rebecca Aidlin

For Dawn

Bright's Passage

1

The baby boy wriggled in his arms, a warm, wet mass, softer than a goat and hairier than a rabbit kit. He held a blade over a candle flame for some time, then cut the cord and rubbed the baby with a wetted shirt. When this was done he laid the child in a basket near the fire and then stood at the head of the bed and looked down at his wife's face a long moment. Abruptly, he bent low and placed his head near her mouth, staying all the while stone silent, waiting for some whisper from her lips. At last he stood straight once more, seeming to disappear into the still blackness of the low rafters as if he had become just another of the cabin's shadows. The child began to cry, and he turned to look at it lying there by the glow of the dying fire.

The man paced the floor, biting the large front knuckle of his fist. At length he picked the child up from its basket and lifted the flap of heavy hide over the doorway, stepping out into the last of the blue twilight as the rising sun began to gild the topmost trees along the crest of the ridge.

Although he'd lived in its shadow almost his whole life, he stood there watching the sleeping leafy hulk closely as if for the first time. The forest was in the full trembling swell of high summer, the trees clamorous for sunlight, permitting only a few stray drops of gold to fall between their leaves and onto the scraggly undergrowth below. The ridge would offer nothing in the way of hindrance should men take it upon themselves to cross it. He again put his hand to his mouth and could be seen from the dark of the nearby chestnut tree to bite down hard on that knob-knuckled, much-abused fist. When the fit had passed he sat down cross-legged on the ground, his crying baby boy in his lap. The child's eyes were shut tightly, but its paw searched the air waveringly for something until the man put his finger down and the little hand grasped it, held it. The two waited there a while.

By and by the angel spoke from the darkness by the chestnut tree. "She's gone."

"Course she's gone! What am I doing out here with the baby if she ain't gone?"

There was silence.

"Yeah," he said after a while, his voice catching, "she's gone."

"That's how it had to be."

"You didn't tell me that she had to die," the man said accusingly. "You said to do whatever you told me to do and you'd keep us safe . . ."

The silence continued for so long that he knew the angel would not answer him, but he continued to sit there anyway, one arm holding the child close while the other arm worked a stick into the packed dirt. The child had red hair and cried and cried.

Nearby, a hutch held several hens clucking pointlessly at one another, and atop the hutch, white against the still-dark trees, stood the she-goat. Without his mother's rifle he had not been able to hunt that winter, and he had been forced to slaughter the goat's kids, and finally the billy, one by one. Now the white little widow stood atop the hutch all day every day, coming down to the dirt only to forage or to be milked.

Even when his wife was hugely pregnant she had milked the she-goat to keep the milk flowing, but yesterday morning her water had broken before she'd had the chance, and the ensuing afternoon and evening had been long and frightful. Now the goat's udder was strained to bursting. He fetched the basket from the cabin, set it on a stump, and laid his son inside it. Then, kneeling by the stream, he washed his hands clean of blood and grime. He rose with much fatigue and made his way slowly across the bedraggled stretch of dirt to the hutch, lifted the goat down, and squeezed the milk into a bucket.

When the bottom of the bucket was covered with milk, he took it to the baby. Dipping his finger in the froth, he held it to the boy's suckling mouth. He sat and fed the baby like this as the last of the dark was drawn away and the dawning sky was revealed, pink and leafed with clouds. When the baby was done eating it seemed to crumble in upon itself, and for a terrible moment he thought that the infant had died, until, by the movement of its tiny fingers, it became clear that the boy was only sleeping.

He went inside and pulled a small black lacquer box off the shelf and from this box removed an ivory comb, yellowed with age and impossibly delicate. The comb's handle was carved in the shape of a kneeling woman, her hands folded in prayer. She wore a long gown with flowers on the fringe, and her hair was plaited into two flowing tresses on either side of her face beneath a tiny crown. It was ancient, this comb, having belonged to his mother and before that to a Queen of England.

He sat near the head of the bed and began to comb the tangles from his wife's hair. She had thrashed all night and the odor of stale sweat hung in the room, mixing with the plummy tang of blood. He spoke softly to her and touched her face often as he ran the comb through her hair, parting it at the scalp and arranging it on either side down her shoulders like the woman on the comb. Then he straightened her body in the bed, arranging her arms across her breasts so that her palms met in an attitude of prayer.

When this was done he took a dead black ember from the fire and, using a nail, mixed it with some of the goat's milk in a tin cup. He pulled the Bible off the shelf, lifted the age-slackened cover of the heavy book, and, using the nail as a quill, beneath the names of long-dead others wrote:

Rachel Bright
1900–1920
Wife of Henry Bright

He lifted the nail from the page and surveyed the grisly black scrawl of the epitaph. Outside, the horse began to slap its tail against the trunk of the chestnut tree. He dipped the nail once more in the ink and added:

Mother to the Future King of Heaven

When this was done he held the Bible open on his knee and read the other names, but, except for his mother and father's and his aunt Rebecca's, they were all strangers to him. As he read, his hand worried absently through the pages and pulled a thistle from between the leaves where it had marked, like new grass over a grave, some passage that had been special to his mother. He looked now for the page, but it was lost to him, and he threw the thistle to the coals.

He went to the cabin door and looked out on the child, then gazed up to the hills again, watching them closely. Nothing but the quantity of the light upon the canvassed green trees had changed. He retrieved the long-handled shovel that he had last used for mucking out the chicken hutch and walked beneath the dark spread of the chestnut tree to where his horse stood.

"Now git," he said. The horse was standing directly above where he wished to bury his wife. "Now *git*," he said again, and pushed himself against the horse's shoulder.

"We have to go from here," said the horse. "We have to take the Future King of Heaven and leave."

"Why?"

"That will be made known to you in due time, Henry Bright. First we have to leave this place. You will burn it down." The horse bent to the patch of timothy grass and pulled up on it, munching with a broad satisfaction.

"Where are we gonna live if we burn it down?" Bright watched the plate-shaped muscles of the big jaws working.

"That will be answered once we leave," said the angel.

Bright's eyes wandered over the cabin he had grown up in. His father had gone away to the coal mines to earn money before Henry was born and had died in a cave-in, leaving his wife to raise their son amid a wilderness of tendrils and gnats that seemed always on the verge of devouring the little house. Much later, after his mother died and Henry had gone off to the War, the chimney had returned itself to the land, becoming a tunnel of vines and birds' nests so thick that the first time he had tried to cook over the fire after he came back, the smoke had driven him outside and the mourning doves had thrown themselves from the eaves to the ground in confused jumbles. Sometimes, as they lay in bed at night, it had seemed to Rachel and him as if the whole cabin was hurtling at great speed through the dark, so loudly did the wind wail through the chinks in the caulking.

"Why do you want me to burn it down?" he asked again. "That's our house. We ain't got any other house."

"Then stay here—"

"My boy needs a roof over his head."

"—and let your son die."

Bright shoved the animal again, to little effect. The horse stood its ground. "We can leave, angel, but I ain't gonna burn it down!" he yelled. "It's all I got left!"

On the stump behind him, the baby began to cry. Bright whirled around, shielding his own tears from the horse's view. He stood with his back to the angel for a long time, his shoulders jerking violently at first and then slowing to a composed rise and fall. He ran the back of a hand across his face and looked at the cabin.

"Henry Bright," the angel said, finally breaking the silence, "do as I say."

The back of Bright's head fell forward as his chin sank to his chest. "I can't believe this," he said. "All right. All right, I'll burn it down."

He ran a hand across his face again and then, turning back, he gave the horse a final push and the animal stubbornly relinquished his ground. Then he set about digging a grave for his wife next to that of his mother. When he was knee-deep in the ground, he heard the baby begin to cry again, and so he climbed up from the hole and moved the basket out of the sunlight. He fed the boy with the goat's milk again and returned to digging. When he had finished the grave, he went inside and cut his wife out of her clothes.

Opening the large trunk, he looked down at what to dress her in. The white dress lay there, its stiff collar holding up determinedly against desperate age and the fungal dampness of high July. He reached beneath this garment to where the slip, with its tiny lace eyelets, waited primly. He had bought the slip for her in Fells Corner, an extravagant wedding gift that was almost the only thing she had worn until she was finally too big with child even for it to fit. It glowed out at him with a spectral whiteness in the ill-lit lowness of the cabin. After that came the brutal, delicate task of getting her stiffening body into the garment, but when he was done he again arranged her beautiful hair on either side of her shoulders, the way he liked it best. Finally, he opened the black lacquer box once more and removed a length of golden ribbon. He tied it around her head like a crown and stood up to survey his work.

He'd dug enough graves to know that she would fit perfectly into this one, but even so he stood there with her body in his arms, a rack of painful hesitation as he considered taking a few planks from the cabin in order to build her a box that would keep her from ending up so dirty.

"There's no time!" the horse nickered behind him, as if it knew his mind, which perhaps it did. "Leave her buried deep and let's go."

He sat at the edge of the grave, his legs hanging into the hole, and dropped her in. He whispered something down at her, then he stood up and began to shovel in the dirt as a preacher might baptize someone in frigid water: quickly, to overcome the shock of the cold. He began to cry again. While he worked, the horse stood nearby, dark and still, perhaps gone to sleep. He filled the grave and then knelt, spreading leaves and sticks over the slight mound. The heat was coming on hard now, and sweat ran over his brow and into his eyes before continuing down his face and neck in the long, dusty canals that had already been carved by his tears.

When he stood up from the grave, he went to the cabin flap and pulled a handful of corn kernels from a sack hanging just inside the doorway where the animals could not get at it. Then he stood in the yard near the chickens. Stock-still, his arms hanging loosely at his sides, he let a few of the kernels fall from between his fingers. The three birds pecked at the kernels and then looked up, pinning him against the sky with their tiny black eyes and waiting for more. He chose the hen he would try for, and when it looked up at him again he let a few more kernels fall. When he and Rachel had been small, they used to play with the chicks in the yard of the elderly couple his mother had cooked for. Rachel liked to hold the little yellow things against the nape of her neck and would laugh as their feathers tickled her. He would lie very still on his back and they would see how many she could put on his chest.

The third time Bright let the kernels fall, the chickens did not look up but busily went about their feeding. He bent quickly, grabbed the hen by its head, and broke its neck. The goat watched on without emotion from atop her perch.

He plucked the body quickly, then went inside and placed it on a spit above the embers of the dying fire. He brought the baby in and laid it on the bed where it might survey the room it was born in. Maybe someday the Future King of Heaven would need to describe his own humble beginnings.

He took off his dirty clothes and put on the uniform that he had worn home from the War. His fingertips touched at the bullet hole in the jacket's shoulder as his eyes searched the cabin for what he would need and what he could carry: a haversack, his woolen blanket and greatcoat, the spare shirt, underclothes, a toothbrush, a cup, matches, a cook skillet, a fork; and his mother's ivory comb. The bucket would hang over the pommel along with the sack of corn. He took a length of fishing line and hooks and tried laying them flat between the pages of the Bible, but upon hefting the heavy book he decided against taking it with him and replaced it on the shelf. He piled the rest of his traveling possessions at the feet of the horse, then looked up at the ridge warily once more, searching the forest for faces. He thought of his mother's rifle, but of course it was gone, so he went back inside and sat in the cabin for the last time, feeding the child with his trigger finger dipped in the goat's milk and waiting for the chicken to finish cooking.

The sun was high above its cradle in the crook of the mountains by the time he was finally ready to depart. The cabin, stripped of his wife and his few possessions, sat there in naked impoverishment, a sorry matchbox devoid even of matches. He had cut the stiff white dress into strips, fashioning the swath that had been its bodice into a sling that he hung around his neck to carry the child. The other strips he had slathered in the grease of the cooked chicken and placed in the corners of the house. He had only a small ration of matches and he had never been the kind to waste a match anyhow, so once he'd placed the rags in the corners of the room, he lit one and carefully carried the guarded flame from one pile to the next until each was aflame. Then he walked out to the yard and stood by his horse to watch the cabin burn.

"It's not going to go."

"It will. I can start a fire without a angel."

"You can't do anything without a angel."

"It'll go," he said. "You watch."

"Get the Bible."

Bright scuffed the ground with a boot. "You're always telling me we don't need the Bible no more! Haven't you been saying that since we met? That the King of Heaven is bad and we need a new one and all that?"

"What you say is true."

"So how'm I supposed to understand you if you keep changing what you say? First we don't need the Bible and now we do?"

"Henry Bright, go back inside and use the Bible to help start the fire. Now."

"Rachel died," he said. He swatted at a fly that was tickling his face.

11

"And you are grieving."

"Yeah." He pulled the child from the basket and put it in the sling around his neck.

"I understand. Now go back in and don't come out until the fire is started."

He stared incredulously at the angel a moment, but the horse just looked placidly ahead at the dark cabin as if waiting for a page to turn. Bright stalked across the dirt yard to the flap, lifted it perfunctorily, and peered inside. The rags sat in the corners of the room, smoking sullenly. He did not look back at the horse but entered the cabin, took the Bible down off the shelf, and began to tear its pages out, crumpling page after page into yellowed knuckles of parchment, finally throwing the ransacked book facedown on the bed when he'd harvested enough. He placed the paper in piles above the smoldering rags and then, twisting a few remaining sheets of Leviticus into a brand, he lit the piles once more.

He rejoined the horse in the yard. It looked at him smugly but said nothing as the dried wood of the cabin popped into flames. Henry Bright bit his fist as the fire took hold. Then, lowering his chin to his chest, he let his eyes rest on the tiny face of his son, the Future King of Heaven.

2

Mud and water and the stumps of trees. In every direction that was all there was. Bodies fell, but the trees died standing up. Nightly they were crucified upon themselves by the zip and whine of machine guns, their leaves corroded by gas, their branches and trunks hacked for kindling, some roots cut by entrenching tools, others drowned by the ceaseless, steady drip-dripping of blood and rain. Back home, these waning days of September could seem at times like one long sunset, the oak and hickory forest a blaze of yellow, orange, and red leaves. Here, it was impossible to tell by the trees what season it was; any that were still standing had nothing left to give away.

They'd been told that the Argonne would remind them of home, but as they'd moved ever closer to the front line, from transport trains to dirt roads to muddy tracks to brutal gashes in the ground, the greenery had disintegrated around them until finally the only tree that Henry Bright could see from where he was squatting in his trench was a barkless and bone-white totem thirty yards distant. This tree, too, had to go, because someone important far back of the line had decided that German gunners must be using it to site their long-range artillery. Perhaps this was so, but the line had been ebbing and flowing around the tree for so long now that it was just as likely that the very same someone important had simply grown tired of looking at it through binoculars all day. Regardless, an order had just come down to Sergeant Carlson that he and three other men were to blow it up when the night was at its pitchest black.

Bright tore a sheet from *The Stars and Stripes* lying nearby where he rested his haunches against the trench wall. He scanned it:

> If we laugh at the cooties when they come, and hunt them with the same merriment that the French hunt the wild boar, the joke will be on them after all, for they do not laugh back. And then they won't seem half so bad. Laughter is a good insecticide!

He cleaned himself as best he could and pulled his britches back up, then made his way down the narrow length of trench to the zag. Here he angled a sharp right, squeezing by a lumpy yellow-haired kid named Bert plodding in the opposite direction. A few moments later he heard the boy turn and slosh through the mud to catch up behind him.

"Hey, what's the idea, Bright? That was a paper for all us boys to read! How long's it gonna last anyway, if everybody comes along and wipes their ass with it?" He waited for an answer from Bright and got none. Bert seemed younger than the rest of the men, or if not younger, at least pinker. He seemed made of pinkness. His father was a banker in Wheeling. Around the next zag, some of the others had finished pulling the sandbags from a portion of the trench wall and were now hollowing out a cavity in which to bury McCauliff and Standish. The two men had been shot by a sniper within a few moments of each other, just before noon. Bert squeezed between Bright and the trench wall, raising his voice so that the men digging could hear him. "So, Bright went and wiped his ass with the newspaper again," he said, as if it was some sort of common occurrence for there to be paper of any kind lying about.

"Who's got paper?" one of the others said. "I need a few pages. Let me see 'em, Bert."

"I need pages too!"

"How'd it stay so dry?"

"This is all that's left," Bert said. "I was too late to save the rest." He waved the unused portion of *The Stars and Stripes* above his head for everyone to see. The paper exploded in his hand as a bullet tore through the pages.

"Jee-roosh!" Bert jerked his arm below the lip of the trench. His eyes were the size and shine of quarters as he looked at the remnants of the newspaper in his hand. He let the scraps fall to the mud and turned dejectedly back down the trench in the direction of the latrine. Everyone else, Bright included, finished burying McCauliff and Standish in the wall of the trench. Then they all sat there waiting for something, or nothing, to happen.

Five hours after darkness fell, they sat in lines against the trench wall and listened to the random fire of ammunition for miles to either side. It began to rain again, though at times star shells would brightly illuminate the ground, as if the moon were making bayonet lunges at the earth. The rain slapped at the soil in weary, unwelcome applause. Finally, Sergeant Carlson heaved himself off the trench wall. Bright and two others did the same, dressing themselves in the dung-colored burlap they wore in order to blend in against the hummocked and devastated ground of the battlefield. They climbed over the top of the trench and out into the open, moving slowly on their bellies as if the slurry of mud and bodies, wire and spent casings, were in reality only a thin layer of ice that might at any moment shatter and fall away into an abyss beneath them.

The dynamite was strapped to Bright's back, and Sergeant

15

Carlson had the fuse on a spool tied to his belt. The other two, just in front of them, had wire cutters. They had blacked their bayonets and entrenching tools over a cook flame so that the metal edges would not glint out of the darkness and give them away to the opposite line. They wore no helmets for the same reason. They would dig small holes at the base of the tree and deposit the dynamite. Then they would unspool the fuse, setting a light to it once they were back in their own trench.

It took almost an hour to cover a distance of thirty yards. There were bodies everywhere, mostly from an earlier failed advance on a group of machine-gun emplacements. After the advance had been repulsed, stretcher bearers from both sides had gone into the field to collect the wounded and had been shot; now the bodies lay there in jumbles to be crawled over. There was much wire to cut, and the ground was cratered hellishly, but at length they reached the tree as the rain began to ease to a drizzle. Carlson untied the bundle of dynamite from Bright's back and handed the first stick to the next man, so that he could in turn hand it to the next man to place in the hole. Bright lay still on his stomach, his arms outstretched in front of him, his body pressed flat against the earth.

In front of him suddenly the air felt strange, and then without warning one of his hands was cupping a face. Its features froze in his hand for an awful moment before whispering something. It whispered again, louder this time, and at the sound of the voice the others around Bright went still. If the alarm was raised on either line guns on both sides would open up.

"Shoosh," the voice said, almost a sigh. The War seemed to fall silent at the voice of the German soldier and darkness lay around it like a pack of bristling, dreaming dogs.

A star shell hissed upward and turned the sky to tin. Bright did not close his eyes. Instead, he looked directly into the eyes of the man's face in his hand. On either side of the face, four

16

other men were also pressed tightly to the ground. The man looked steadily back into Bright's eyes as the light flared and then subsided.

"Shoosh," Sergeant Carlson himself whispered after a dark age. He said it calmly, and it was returned calmly, the word bouncing quietly around in the darkness until Bright felt the face in his hand speak it as well once more. He pulled away and the party pushed back from the tree, Sergeant Carlson unspooling the fuse as they retreated. Bright made out the scuffle of fabric and the soft tink of metal as the soldiers on the other side did likewise. Less than an hour later, back in the trench, Carlson and the other two men smoked and talked lowly while Bright sat on a wet duckboard and stared at the nothingness of the trench wall.

"Jee-roosh!" Bert, who hadn't gone, said to no one in particular.

They waited perhaps ten minutes more and then Carlson lit the fuse. Even as he did, though, the tree exploded up into the night sky with a tremendous crack. A second and third blast told them that the German dynamite had gone off. They listened to the hooting of the men across the field, and watched their own fuse crawl like a lost lightning bug over the ground, finally detonating its charges beneath the wrecked stump of the tree.

3

Henry Bright had seen many buildings burn in France during the War, but this did not seem to lessen his surprise at the sudden gusts of heat that washed over him and his newborn boy as the cabin blossomed into flames. The roof shingling was first to catch, blazing upward with terrifying speed. The incendiary heat quickly consumed this kindling, and the remainder of the roof collapsed down inside the thick log walls of the cabin, throwing sparks and burning pieces of wood into the air as it did so. The she-goat, who had not been to the War but had earned, by any honest estimation, a hard-won reputation for composure in the last several months, lost the last reserves of her calm and burst out with a serrated bleat of alarm. She tugged against her tether as the horse canted back onto its hind legs in fright. Bright struggled to hold the leads of both animals as he watched the sparks climb into the air. Then it seemed that even the fire caught fire. In the space of a few moments there were three smaller blazes burning at the periphery of the farmyard, one of which had begun to crawl over the chicken hutch on its way toward the graves of his wife and mother. He tried to rush forward in order to stomp out the blaze, but the leads by which he held his frightened livestock were far too short and he could not reach the fire without letting the animals go. The peripheral branches of the big chestnut tree began to wither and brown, falling to the ground like burning feathers. The young chestnuts popped in their spiky shells, exploding in the angry swell of heat. Then, with a howl, the whole tree was aflame.

"What the hell did you make me do!?" Bright shouted at the angel over the roar, but the horse was twisting and stamping at the ground and would not answer. Bright gave a tremendous pull on its lead. The horse fought him for a few seconds, dancing in panic as the goat darted this way and that. He finally got the horse around somehow, tugging it and the goat into the cool safety of the woods to the east.

There was a short rise half a mile away, and he tied the animals to a tree and walked to the top. A steady floral breeze was blowing at his back and had already pushed the fire below from the chestnut tree to a silver maple nearby. The wood burned in a plume of viscous, greasy heat that shot into the sky like a column of dirty water. He turned and walked back down the rise, the familiar, low rumble of combustion beginning its muttering in his ears.

He did not speak as he untethered the horse and goat from the tree, and the horse, for its part, allowed itself to be ridden into the depths of the woods without a struggle. For all its earlier shows of panic, it now seemed deaf to the buzzing alarm that was spreading through the forest canopy. For the next few miles it clomped along with the maddening contentedness of an old dray taking the pumpkins to town. Once or twice it tried to chomp at the clumps of grass along its path, but Bright pulled back sharply on the reins each time, cursing the angel under his breath.

"Last time I let a goddamn angel help me start a goddamn fire," he said. "He makes fun of me, tells me I can't start a fire without a angel, and then that very angel goes and burns the whole goddamn forest down." He rode along in silence for a

19

piece more. "Goddamn it," he added. A voluptuous purple-headed thistle drew the horse off to the right, but Bright jerked it back.

"It was you who started the fire, Henry Bright, not me."

"It's gonna burn the whole goddamn forest! Ain't you gonna do something?"

"What can I do?"

"It was you told me to set it. Now you don't know what to do with it?"

"I didn't tell you to set the whole forest on fire, only the cabin," the horse sighed as it ambled along. "Sadly, there's no stopping it now. But have heart, Henry Bright."

"But ain't the Colonel going to see the smoke? You know he will."

"I know he will."

Bright pulled back on the reins and the horse came to a stop. "You do?"

"Of course I do. I know everything, Henry Bright."

"But we don't want him to see the smoke, I thought. 'Cause he'll know something's on fire and he'll come over the mountain, him and his boys."

"And what will they find?"

Bright looked down at his own son, who had stopped crying for the moment. "He won't find nothing, because the whole goddamn forest is gonna be burned down," he said.

"And what will the Colonel and his sons think then?"

"That we're dead. Both me and Rachel," he said. "Burned up in the fire."

"And your son?"

"Him too. They'll think he's dead too." He bit his fist. "Do you think they'll really think that? That we all just got burned up in the fire?"

"The fire started in the early morning while you and your

wife were still asleep. By the time the conflagration had passed over, there was nothing to show that you or she and her unborn child had ever existed. It was a tragedy."

"And you think they'll believe that? The Colonel is gonna believe that?"

"Why would he not?"

"Well, for one thing, he's had Corwin and Duncan watching us."

"How do you know?"

"'Cause I saw them. Up on the ridge in the winter, when there was no leaves on the trees. They were just sitting there looking at me one time. And then even last week I saw Duncan. He was on his belly there in the shadows underneath the ferns by the side of the road. I think the Colonel was waiting for my boy to be born. I think he wants to take my boy away from me."

The angel said nothing to this and Bright mused a while in the saddle, rolling the terrible notion in his mind. The horse made another foray, this time into a stand of nettles, and Bright, lost in his reverie, permitted it.

They rode on for several more hours, the light shifting and dappling, the humidity settling around them like a warm, wet sigh, until at length they came to a rill and followed it down a long hillside to where it emptied itself into a fast-running stream. Here they stopped and he removed the baby from the sling around his chest and placed it on the ground. He stripped off his shirt, and, dipping both shirt and sling in the cool water, he rubbed the fabrics together until the mess the boy had made was gone. The baby wailed as he dunked its hindquarters in the flow, but it quieted some after he laid it upon the woolen blanket. By the time he had milked the goat, the last portion of sunlight was being sopped up by the low moon, and the stars were beginning to show on the plate beneath. He tied the horse to a chokecherry and the goat to a peeling ninebark near the water.

21

It was muggy, but he unpacked his greatcoat anyway and, sitting on the ground, wrapped himself and the child in the garment, more for relief from the mosquitoes than from any cold. With his finger, he fed the boy from the milk and with his other hand ate a piece of the chicken that he'd wrapped in a few pages from the Book of Jeremiah. Then Henry Bright lay back and thought about Rachel, the delicate shells of her ears, the pinkness of her tongue, the way she laughed in her sleep. The tiny body of his son slept silent and warm in the crook of one arm, and he kept very still lest he should wake the boy.

4

With the tree gone, the world went aimless for the next several days. Shots were taken at whatever happened to rise above the bags that lined the trenches, but even the bodies of the men who were hit seemed bored by the tedium of the killings and fell to the ground with more listlessness than violence. Of course there were always the punctual, workmanlike exchanges of shelling, shooting, and maiming, called "the hate," at the beginning and ending of each day, but by now these were ritual, and no one paid them much mind.

Bright's company was relieved and went to sit in the dirty basements of eviscerated villages under the watchful eyes of old women. Everyone had fleas. Bert argued with whoever would listen to him, mostly about whether chickens could get the cooties. Finally someone had gone out in the yard and killed a bird, brought it in, and inspected it. There had been no fleas. Behind a basket of onions in a nook that served as a kitchen, Bright found a small patch of plaster wall so white that it seemed supernatural, a solitary untouched thing in the whole wet and muddy world. He stared hard at it while the others smoked cigarettes and slept around him. They were moved from the basement back to the reserve trenches, and he resumed watching the treeless early October sky with the same intensity as he had the wall in the old woman's house. Shells burst around him, but they burst around everyone. Many had caught the flu, and there was coughing at all hours. Some suffocated in the night from the infection in their lungs. Men came back from the field hospitals looking sicker than when they had left for them. They died of fevers in the cold, their bodies shivering so violently beneath sodden blankets that it seemed their bones might break. It was not unusual to wake and find the man sitting next to you dead; the War had become something so powerful that it could kill without wounding. On occasion even Henry Bright smoked, but not often.

Back he moved to the front line, and, one morning, the hate was louder and longer than normal, and he began to clean his rifle with his toothbrush and then fix his bayonet in preparation to go over the bags. The word being passed around was that the village in front of them had been relinquished in the night. Some speculated that it was a trap, that this portion of the line was playing possum, luring in as many as they could in order to surround them in one last, desperate attempt to turn the tide of the War. Farther south, another rumor had it, an entire German company of starving old men and young boys had surrendered en masse. Some held that this would be the final push, that the Kaiser had had it and the German army was collapsing. Still, if this was the case, no one in charge was saying so, and until they did say so, the only thing that mattered was the village that lay before them a little ways distant, close enough that the white steeple of its church could be seen peeking out above a small rise of hills.

His mother had died during a windstorm that made the trees bow to one another like ballroom dancers. He had buried her in the whipping rain and then trudged through the mud to Fells Corner for nails with which to patch the holes where the singles had blown off the cabin's roof. The hardware man had measured out the nails, offered his condolences, and then asked Bright if he'd considered signing up to go to the War. The hardware man had been made a registration officer with the responsibility of signing up men to go across the sea to avenge the women and children of the *Lusitania,* to make the world safe for Democracy, to defend France, and, lastly, to aid England. With his mother dead, there was nothing really to stay for. Bright had signed his name, listened wordlessly to the instructions the man gave him, and then headed back to the cabin with an extra portion of nails for being the first to sign up in the book. It had been as easy as falling in a river.

In early March 1918, he hid his mother's rifle in the rafters above the bed, used the extra portion of nails to cover the door frame against the weather and wilderness, and then walked to the train depot in Fells Corner. He was mustered at a camp in Virginia with a company of gangly and goosenecked men and boys. By late April they were on their way to France.

Feeling for the War was high, as was excitement over the ocean voyage. Men showed it in different ways. Some told stories of their valor in advance. Others prayed and gave up vices. Most wrote letters of some kind to be mailed home upon their arrival, and a chaplain assigned to their unit tried to get everyone's soul in order. He was most concerned about the Catholics of France. "You stay the hell out of those churches, boys," he would shout as they went to sleep. "You just walk the other way. There ain't nothing those Catholics can give you except fleas and the clap. You need anything, you want to unburden your soul, you come to me or you go to the YMCA." He was naturally red in the face and, according to Sergeant Carlson, accidentally shot himself during a training exercise, only two weeks after their boat had landed in France.

They entered the War like men stepping out from beneath an awning into a torrential thunderstorm. The first man that Bright saw die fell back down into the very trench from which he'd just climbed. His uniform was still fresh and the tops of his boots had been shined. Only the soles looked muddy.

5

Bright rode on throughout the next day, following the stream and keeping to the hug of a range of foothills where the canopy of hickory was thickest and there was less chance of being seen. He took short breaks to water the horse and to feed the child from the thin skim of goat's milk in the bucket tied to the saddle pommel. As the sun began to slip behind him, he tethered the horse near an ess in the stream. A few deep-brown trout grazed fatly in the dark holds beneath a stretch of half-submerged hemlock trunk that had fallen across the water. He unswaddled his son, walked out on the trunk with the boy, and knelt down as he had done the previous night to dunk the boy's naked hindquarters in the water. The child meeped and mewed up at him as he laid it on the ground. He walked out onto the trunk once again to wash the diaper, but this time as he stooped to the stream he lost his balance and toppled headfirst into the water. He stood up spluttering, thoroughly soaked, and, reaching into his pocket, found the matches ruined.

He stood there, waist-deep and dripping, looking down into his palm at them. Then he let them fall from his hand to float away like tiny boats in the current. He sloshed through the churned silt to the steep lip of the bank and pulled himself up next to his boy. The child's feathery red hair fell thinly across its knobbled head in the style of a middle-aged auctioneer or feed-store man. The same coppery color gave the boy a pair of sharp little eyebrows that scrunched and relaxed and then scrunched again as if, behind those tightly locked eyelids, he was figuring a sum of arithmetic. The intricacy of the boy's ears and the translucence of his tiny nostrils already bore the stamp of Rachel's beauty. His face was so unlike the faces of the infants Bright had seen frolicking among the painted clouds of a certain church back in France. It was a good, open face, without malevolence or mischief. Bright rolled onto his back and regarded the sweeping trees above. At length he pulled himself to his feet, stripped naked, and hung his clothes up on some low-hanging branches to dry.

When the father and son returned to camp, the horse took one look at Henry Bright's pale, stem-thin body and snorted. Bright ignored the animal and set about clearing a patch of ground, arranging the woolen blanket, and laying the child upon it. Next he set the goat loose and watched her forage, by which way she led him to a mulberry bush, a serviceberry bush with a few precious berries that had somehow escaped the notice of the birds, and a gnarled old crab apple tree, loaded down with tight, bitter green fruit. He ate with as little compunction as the goat. He had fishing line, but without matches there would be no campfire. Perhaps that was just as well; another fire, one that might betray their whereabouts to the Colonel and his sons, could be even more disastrous than the fire the angel had made him set in order to burn the cabin down. He ate the unripe crab apples and milked the goat, feeding the boy from the bucket and leaving aside a good portion from which to feed him again in the night when the child awoke hungry.

As Bright made ready to sleep, the horse's derisive humor descended into contempt. It stared darkly from out of a purple and malignant silence as Bright curled his naked form closely around his son. The boy muzzled into Bright's chest. Bright noticed the angel's scornfulness, and though he said nothing, he stared back at the horse from the darkness with a like animus.

He sat up again suddenly. "What did you call me?"

The horse chuffed the air. "What do you mean?"

"You called me something." Bright flicked the ground with his hand. "You wanna call me names, you just say 'em loud enough for me to hear 'em."

"You are mistaken, Henry Bright."

Bright whipped his jacket over his child's nakedness and then, with a final deathly stare, he rolled over to face away from the animal. Around them in the forest thrummed the ordinary night sounds, but beneath those came the ossiary click as Henry Bright's jaws worked to eat the sounds deep down in his throat that might betray his great grief at the death of his wife, his foolhardy destruction of their home, and the wildfire that had ensued. He thought fearfully of being discovered in the night by the Colonel and his cruel sons and, as he bit the knuckles of his fist, the bitterness of the crab apples he had eaten mixed against his tongue with the sour shame of being mocked by his own horse.

6

"You said we were going to be married?" Rachel asked expectantly out of the darkness. She sat in front of him astride the horse as they left the Colonel's house behind.

"We will," Bright said.

"Oh, good. I hate this thing." She began to tear at her ragged white dress. A bundle of thread tangled out from the shoulder, where a bow had once blossomed. On the other shoulder the bow was still hanging on, but it drooped lifelessly. "Can't wait to get it off." By the motion of her arm he could tell that she was tugging the dirty stretch of silk that ran between her neckline and her breasts.

"Don't you tear at that thing," he said, letting go of the horse's rein to pull her arm down and her hand away from the garment. "We ain't married yet and I ain't got nothing else for you to wear."

"So?"

"So, you can't get married naked, can you? When was the last time you ever heard of anyone getting married naked?"

She giggled at this, as if he hadn't just ridden his horse through the front door of the Colonel's house and stolen her away. "Are we going to get married real soon?" she asked again.

"I said we were, didn't I? Didn't I just tell you that?"

"Real, real soon, then?" There came a ripping sound, and a scrap of white fabric floated to the ground. The horse snorted.

Bright brushed the girl's hands away from her dress once more. "Yes. Now stop tearing at that. Take your hands away and stop messing with it!"

Dawn was breaking as they melted out of the darkness of the woods and into the tenuous circle of habitation that he had reclaimed from the wilderness in the month since he'd returned from the War.

She got down from the horse and stood in the center of it all, surveying the little farmyard expectantly as Bright looped the animal's tether loosely around the chestnut tree and then went to the stream to dunk his head in the water. He came up gasping from the cold.

"You might want to wash yourself too," he said, rubbing an arm across his forehead as he looked at her. "Get cleaned up a bit." The girl stood where she was. He disappeared into the cabin and came back with a clean shirt on.

"You ain't washed up yet," he said. "You're filthy, girl. Goddamn." In the morning light the girl's face and hands had lost the marble whiteness with which they'd glowed in the gloom of the previous evening.

"Stay there," he said. "I'm going to get the Bible. Will you stay right there?"

"I'll stay. I'll stay right here with this tired old horse. He's a nice horse. Aren't you a nice horse?" She reached up to scratch the animal's ears.

"You don't need a Bible," the horse said. "Come here and stand near the bride."

He immediately turned around and came to stand near Rachel.

"I thought you were going to get the Bible," she said.

"We don't need it."

31

"Ask the bride her name."

"Her name's Rachel!" he burst out. "You know that's her name! She's all you been talking about!" Then, remembering that she was standing right there beside him, he ducked his chin to his chest and looked at her bare feet. "I been talking about you to my horse," he said, forcing a chuckle out.

"You have?" The girl giggled as she stroked the horse's head.

"You must ask the girl her full name. This is a sacred ceremony."

"For God's sake." Bright stomped a foot on the ground.

"What?" Rachel asked.

"Nothing." Bright sighed. "What's your name, Rachel? Your full name, is what I mean."

"It's Miss Rachel Stallsworth Murtry Marion Morse," she said, and then, unaccountably, "On account of us being Catholic on the Lady Stallsworth's side."

"What does that mean?" he asked, perhaps to the horse and perhaps to the girl.

"I don't know," the girl said.

The horse said nothing.

"Well, now it's Bright and you're my wife, unless somebody has problems with that," he said significantly, "somebody who makes me go all over the country riding up inside other people's houses, and stealing people's daughters." He spoke expectoratingly into the big face of the horse.

The animal ran its velvet muzzle along the pale floe of the girl's collarbone and paid Bright no mind.

"Well," he said, putting his hands on his hips, "you gonna forever hold your peace, or what?"

The horse snuffled with evident pleasure in the girl's scraggled hair. The girl shied flirtatiously from its attentions.

Bright burrowed his eyes like bullet holes into the animal as it tossed its head for the girl's amusement. After a long moment of silence, he continued. "All right. Then I guess we're married now."

He took Rachel by the hand and pulled her away from the lecherous animal's ears mid-scratch. "Over there"—he motioned toward the cabin—"is where we live. There's where the chickens live. You always been good with them. Those are the goats. This here is a beaten-down old farm horse with no sense in it at all." He was about to point out the stream but she had already begun walking toward it, not even stopping as she pulled the dress over her head and let it fall forgotten on the bank. Then she was wriggling in the icy water. When she stood, the water halfway up her calves, Henry Bright looked upon her naked body for the first time. She bent her head to the stream, dunking it, and then straightened, looking frankly at him as she twisted the water from her hair.

7

You were never to run when advancing. You were to move at a slow and steady pace that allowed the artillery behind you to fire over your head and clear the way for you. Of course, when the ground at your feet exploded it was impossible to tell whether the barrage was coming from in front of you or behind you, so you forgot about slowly advancing and you ran, you ran right into the gun barrels of whoever was there in front of you.

When the order was given, the men climbed the lip of the trench and were soon running across the field. There was always much screaming when this happened, and even Bright would find his mouth hanging open and releasing sounds that he could never quite catch up with and that he could never quite remember afterward. He never looked down no matter what he felt himself stepping on. The fields in between the trenches were wind-whipped ponds of bodies, and even though the bodies were dead they could still pull you down with them; the dead were hungry that way. This morning, with the white beacon of the church in the distance marking the location of the village toward which they were to advance, he climbed out from behind the bags and ran keening and lurching across the dead world of cold limbs and helmets and faces with forgotten names. He had done this before, but this time something felt different. To either side men should have been falling by now. Instead, two had gotten tangled in the barbed wire and a third was frantically trying to cut them loose with a wire cutter. Bright continued on, expecting at any moment to be shot, but as he got ever closer and was not cut down, it became evident that the trenches that lay between them and the village had been surrendered.

After the ragged and slapdash improvisation of their own dwellings, the deserted German trenches were a wonder to behold. Cut much deeper into the ground than the American and French ones, they were reinforced against the shifting mud with concrete. There was a regularity to their construction as well, as if they had been designed dispassionately by some crisp gray architect rather than a panicked animal with a short shovel. A man of average height could almost stand upright in a few of the rooms, and the German soldiers who lived in them, far below the clamor of artillery barrages above, must have experienced, in quieter moments, the same placid satisfaction that brown trout feel as they dream away far beneath the rain-addled surface.

Uniform artillery gaps between the sandbags afforded a clear view of the cavitied village in front of them. The little cluster of buildings seemed far less worthy of defense than the snug bunkers that Henry Bright and his companions now found themselves in.

They scoured the trench for souvenirs but there was little left to take. A couple of large skillets had been abandoned, their weight disqualifying them as items to accompany rapid retreat. There were indecipherable books and a few utensils. Bright was holding an empty cracker tin when a shot rang out. Twenty yards off the trench cut sharply left, then right. Rounding the turn, he saw a wooden door that had swung wide from the trench wall. He crept up to it and, peering around the doorway, found himself looking directly down the black pupil of a pistol barrel. He squeezed the trigger of his own gun reflexively, firing a bullet into the ground between Bert's feet.

"Whoa, Bright! Whoa!" Bert said. "It's me! It's me!" He lowered the pistol he had been pointing at Bright. "Jee-roosh! You trying to kill me or what?"

Three others came around the corner, rifles at the ready. Bright set his own down and sagged back against the trench wall, rubbing his knees and breathing deep.

"It's all right, boys!" Bert called out. "Bright's got an itchy trigger finger is all! Hey, look! I got one! An officer!" Behind him in the room was a man in a wooden swiveling office chair, his head thrown back, his mouth drawn open as if in mid-snore. There was a hole blasted in the side of his head and another one in his stomach.

Carlson pushed through the others in the narrow doorway. "What the hell happened?"

"I came round this corner and found the door open," Bert said. "I crept on up and this big Fritzy in the chair here had his pistol pointed at me. He had a bead on me but I was faster, yessir, I was! I blew him away before he had the chance to pull the trigger!" He held up the officer's pistol that he'd pointed at Bright. "And just look at this! Jee-roosh!"

Carlson took a look at the dead man. "Christ, Bert. How long was this fella dead before you killed him?"

Bert purpled. "You saying I'm lying, Sergeant? You saying I didn't shoot this Fritzy?"

"No. You shot him, Bert." The sergeant started to laugh. "You shot him for sure." He turned to Bright, still leaning leadenly against the trench wall. "You all right?" he asked. Bright nodded his head and took a cigarette one of the other men offered him. "Christ," Carlson sighed finally. "I wish I could be there when you tell this story, Bert." He pushed back through

36

the group of soldiers, and one by one they all turned and followed him up the trench. After a moment Bright, too, stood and made his way to rejoin the others, leaving Bert to stand alone in the doorway, eyes downcast, absentmindedly swinging the officer's pistol at his side.

A short time later the bells in the village church tower began to peal. Bright and the others climbed from the trench and made their way through a pocket of eerie calm toward the clanging. Almost every building had been reduced to rubble. A few thick arches were still standing, and here and there perched the precarious remnants of rooftops, their jagged beams exposed like broken bones. Rising above the chaos of the ruined town, however, stood the church, miraculously spared, its slender steeple chastely white and incongruous with the garish tolling coming from within. A handful of pebble-eyed women and children hid in the shadows, peering out at the new arrivals as they made their way across the town square and toward the source of the bells.

8

Bright lay awake and tried to listen through the night sounds for the vengeful tread of boots. Instead, he was almost sure that he heard the fire, rumbling so low and far off that perhaps it was only the blood rushing in his temples. The baby awoke three times in the night, and each time Bright sat up and rocked the boy in his arms and nursed him with his finger dipped in the goat's milk. The horse stirred where it was tethered and he could see the luminous white goat sleeping beneath the leaves of a bush. He drifted off near dawn, the few clouds overhead blown in mare's tails and limned with an orange light.

He got up sometime later, took up his child and gathered his animals, and continued following the stream that babbled its way eastward at a playful splash, oblivious to Bright's exhaustion and wary sorrow. A little after noon, in a dark green chasm far beneath a railroad trestle, they came across a group of naked young boys swimming in a cauldron made from the large rocks that had tumbled down the mountain and into the stream.

The boys were taking turns swinging on a rope far out into the deep pool. They pretended to ignore Bright while he watered his horse and changed and fed the baby. He set the goat free from its tether and the animal jumped off the bank and into the water, swiping its hooves to keep its head above the slow, glassy current. It swam in several tight circles before clambering up on a large rock that rose above the flow. From here it looked defiantly back at Bright, as the boys smiled like he was some kind of circus man.

While Bright waited for the goat to come back, one of the boys swam across and stood a ways off from him in the water, eyeing Bright's uniform. "Were you in the War?" he asked.

"I was."

"Did you ever kill anybody ever?"

"Yes."

The boy was quiet and looked back over his shoulder at his companions, who made a great show of not returning their friend's glances. The boy turned to face Bright again and shivered, crossing his arms over his bony chest. "Want some blackberries?"

"Can you tell me where a town is at?"

"Why," the boy brightened with his trove of information, "town is just over back that way." He swung an arm over his shoulder, his eyes never leaving Bright's own. "You can't miss it."

"Can you help me fetch my goddamn goat down off that rock?"

The boy smiled a wide, gap-toothed smile. "Sure!" He spun in the water and began to wade deeper, before turning back. "How many Germans did you kill anyways?" he asked, squinting against the glare.

"We won, didn't we?"

9

The Colonel stood at the lip of the grave and looked down at the body of his only daughter, Rachel. He was quiet for a long time. "Well," said Corwin, his fat son, "that's that." The Colonel continued to say nothing. The black embers of the ground squeaked beseechingly beneath his boots as he shifted. Behind him were the charred remains of the cabin where his daughter had died in childbirth. In front of him, across the grave, stood the glass-black trunk of a chestnut tree from which the wildfire had begun its gallop eastward. He looked back down at his daughter. Buried deep, her body had escaped the blaze, and now her skin and the ivory-white slip that she was dressed in dazzled out like a diamond from its soot-black facet of ground.

"Well, that's that," Corwin said again.

"That," said the Colonel, not lifting his eyes from the hole, "is not that. That is your sister. A year ago she was stolen from me and gotten with child. That she is now dead is an insult that will be answered for."

"That's what I meant," Corwin said. "I meant that it was an insult."

Duncan, the Colonel's other son, stood at the head of the grave and looked down. All the way up the ridge from their home, Corwin had been whacking the crystallized black stems of burnt wildflowers, while Duncan trailed silently behind him, a wraith floating over landscape that seemed to have been rendered down into shadows by the flames.

"I told you she was dead," Corwin said to his father. He pushed the shaft of the shovel handle at his brother's chest. Duncan's eyes were the same coal color as his hair. He looked long at Corwin before resettling his gaze on his sister.

His boys had at first dug up the wrong grave. After an hour, the Colonel had stood at the edge of the hole and looked down at the long-dead bones of the rogue's mother. He'd taken the shovel and swung it at his sons for their idiocy. Then, winded, he'd sat down and waited as they dug up his daughter.

The embers he stood upon took to shrieking again as the Colonel turned and looked east, where smoke colored the sky.

"After he buried her, he set the cabin on fire," Duncan said.

The old man looked down at his daughter. "I should have killed him sooner. The many times that I could have shot him down."

"You didn't have any bullets, though."

"In the winter when he went to fetch wood. The days he took the horse to town. When he came out each morning to break the ice from the stream for water. So many times." He shook his head and ground his front teeth. "I let him live, after all. I put aside killing him so that I could do it when his child was born, so that he could see me steal his child, like he stole mine." He turned away from the hole.

"But you couldn't a done it, 'cause you didn't have no bullets."

The Colonel swung aimlessly at Corwin, but he was distracted. "It was vanity," he said. "He would be dead now save for my own vanity. Cover her up."

Duncan began pushing the dirt back into the grave. His eyes were set far back in his head, his thoughts set back even farther.

The Colonel walked up to the top of the rise and surveyed the plumes of smoke as if they came from the camps of some mighty army. To the north ran ridge upon ridge of unbroken forest, but off to the south, where these crenulations began to broaden and grow larger, a silver thread of railroad track stretched east and west, glinting out like a necklace along the nape of the mountainsides. The Colonel came back down the slope to find his sons waiting, sweaty and sullen, by the freshly filled hole.

10

Rachel doted on that mangy old horse. She searched out tart wild apples, brought it thistles and fistfuls of stinging nettles and mint from downstream where the ground turned marshy. As September oranged into October and such treats became harder to find, she would harry Bright for bags of sweet dried corn when he went to town so that she might hold handfuls of it lovingly under the horse's greedy snout. Sometimes, in the wood-smoke-blue mornings, he would watch her leaning against its warm flank, one arm thrown up and across its withers, whispering into its ear as she ran his mother's ivory comb through the animal's forelock. Despite all the girl's attentions, however, the horse's thickening pelt took on a shagged and greasy appearance that, along with its baleful gaze and consumptive ribs, made it look like some moss-covered mule wandered in from a fairy tale.

"She spoils you and I don't know what for," he said to the back of the horse's head one early morning after the first frost. "I don't know what kind of hold you got on her." Horse and man were on the road to Fells Corner for supplies and dried corn. "And don't pretend you don't hear me, 'cause I know you hear me." He twitched the reins pettishly.

"Henry Bright, you have a beautiful wife."

"I know it. I married her, didn't I?"

"No need to sound so jealous. I helped you, so it is only right that you should share her with me."

"Helped nothing!" Bright laughed bitterly atop the animal. "I had to *drag* you inside that goddamn house, remember? If you were gonna steal her and marry her on your own, you coulda done it the minute you thought of it, and with my blessing too, but you couldn't, could you? You don't even have no hands! What if there was a doorknob or something?"

"Henry Bright . . ." The angel affected to sound weary.

"Keep it," Bright snapped. "I'm telling you whatever sweet-talking you're doing to my wife, quit it. She don't need those kinds of distractions right now. We're gonna have a baby."

"The child has been conceived."

"That's what I said, isn't it? So quit whatever other mischief you got on your mind for her and remember the promise that you made to me."

"Which was?" The horse's steaming breath swirled numinously around its ears in the cold air.

"Which *was* that you were gonna keep her and the baby safe from the Colonel and his boys like you done for me in the War. Remember when you said all that? That you'd protect us and the Future King of Heaven and all that?"

"When did it happen?"

"What?"

"When was the child conceived?"

"What the hell does that matter? It got conceived, didn't it? Don't try to change the subject. You gonna keep your promise to me or what?"

"We have done well."

"What do you mean, 'We'?"

The angel said nothing but clomped along thoughtfully.

"Angel?" Bright snapped the reins. "Angel, what do you

mean by 'We'? You ain't done nothing yet. Angel?" Receiving no answer, he sprang from the saddle and stood in the horse's path, bringing it to a desultory halt before him. "I'd hit a horse," he said. "You probably think I wouldn't, but I would."

The two stood there on the empty forest road, their eyes locked. Finally Bright resumed his place in the saddle and they continued on toward town.

"So fearful," the angel tsked.

"Yeah, well, it's your fault if I am. We're in trouble now," Bright said. "I hope you know what you got us into."

"Trouble?" the horse chuckled softly. "From the old man? From his half-wit sons?"

Bright bit his knuckle. "The things those boys did in that house over there in the War." He shivered in the cold air. "It wasn't half-wits that did all that."

"Which is why it could not have been the Colonel's sons."

"Course it was them!" he said, though he spoke under his breath, almost to himself. "I know it was. I *know* it was them." Bright twisted in the saddle and looked back down the road in the direction of the cabin. He scanned the forest to either side of the road for faces. The motley fall curtain of leaves drifted and swelled in the breeze, but none were revealed.

"I told you to close your eyes as the figures approached you where you lay. How then did you see their faces?"

"I opened them while they were standing above me."

"In the darkness?"

"It was getting to be day—"

"Come now, Henry Bright."

"What?! I'm telling you, it was *them*. Duncan stuck his fingers in my mouth to see if I was still alive, remember?"

"How do you know it was Duncan with your eyes closed in the dark?"

"It wasn't dark!"

45

"It was pitch dark and you know it."

"His fingers."

"You knew it was Duncan by his fingers?"

"They're skinnier than Corwin's. Corwin has those big fat fingers."

"I see."

"Oh, why don't you shut up!" He kicked the horse with his heels. "You ain't blind. You seen how fat Corwin's fingers are." He shivered again at the thought of Duncan's bony fingers in his mouth. "They knew I was alive, but they let me live. I think they let me live 'cause they wanted to torture me later. I told you about the other things those boys used to do when we were kids." He snapped the reins curtly against the horse's neck to dispel the memory. "You were there in the ditch with me, angel. You saw it all happen. You ain't gonna make me think I'm crazy."

"You really think it was them," the angel stated flatly.

"I'm telling you, it was!"

"Well, then, half-wits or not, you should be happy that upon your return from the War I told you to save Rachel from them."

"Yeah, yeah. But it's me the Colonel's gonna come kill, not some angel. Must be nice being you! All you get these days is apples and corn and I get nightmares about what them boys did over there in France." His face turned red and he spluttered, "And I tell you what else, I bet that if the Colonel and those boys came down over the ridge today and did to us what they did to those people in that farmhouse during the War, all you'd have to do would be disappear and it wouldn't be no bother to you no more. You'd be just fine, wouldn't you, angel?"

"Peace," the angel said. "They won't come today."

"How do you know that?"

"Shush."

"Don't you shush me!"

"Shush."

11

The boys fetched the goat off the rock in the stream and, shortly after, the baby slung securely around his chest and his livestock in tow, Henry Bright climbed the incline of shale and slate tailings to the road and struck out toward the town to buy a new box of matches. He'd been riding only a few minutes when he heard the growl of an automobile coming around the curve of the mountainside. It swerved to avoid them and then was gone around the next bend, a buff-colored, open-topped blur, its tires spraying his face with bits of gravel, the chemical fumes of its engine exhaust settling in his nose a moment before being picked up by the wind and blown behind him, out across the gorge, through the slats of the railroad trestle and into the sky where it would eventually join with the great veil of smoke that was rising from the forest at his back.

A while later the road changed from gravel to macadam, and the smell of roast chicken and chives, of mint and fresh-baked bread, threaded the air as he and his son rode through drowsing afternoon heat into the town. It seemed a tidy place of dappled white houses and American flags, and he found it almost impossible to keep the greedy animals back from the banquet of flowers spilling down to the street from arbor after shady arbor. Children could be heard, as could the lovely low hum of leisurely work being done: painting of fences, canning of tomatoes and runner beans, gossip over cooling pies. Even the trees here seemed to have a kind of deep green and prepossessing prosperity that the trees of the forest could have no share in.

He found Main Street and tethered the horse and goat under the sign of the general-merchandise store. Inside was long and narrow, and he stood with the baby on his chest in the doorway a moment, allowing his eyes to adjust to the cool darkness of the aisles. The boards under his feet had been worn to a honey luster by workboots and linseed oil. To his left, a long counter supported an ornate brass register, behind which bolts of colored fabric stood row on row. In front of the till, amid a dawdling, noisy clutch of hip-high children, a young woman with a round milky-white face listened to an older woman address the little ones from behind the counter with an auntly air.

Bright walked down the far aisle, listening to their talk, his son sleeping warm against his chest. As he approached with his new box of matches, the two women broke off their conversation and the younger began to arrange her children about her. He laid the matches down on the counter alongside a dime.

The girl turned toward him. "Oh! What a beautiful baby!"

Bright made no reply but tilted his chin down against his chest to peer in acknowledgment at the infant who was just now waking and thrusting tiny fists aimlessly at the air. She pulled back the edge of the sling on his chest to peek in at the boy. "Hello . . . hello," she cooed.

"I believe he needs a diaper," the auntly one said, crinkling her nose. A bleached and sparkling rag appeared off the shelf from somewhere behind her and the woman laid it on the counter, pulling its edges taut and trim with the expert grace of long service. Next, she reached across and lifted the boy from Bright's chest. After undoing the esoteric knots of his own efforts, she laid the child flat on the pristine square of fabric and looked the baby over, pinching a foot, pulling its arms to full extension, clucking first to the right and left of the boy's ears, and finally looking straight down into its tightly closed face. The boy twisted on his back like an overturned turtle. "Few mosquito bites," she said, nuzzling its belly. All at once she tilted her head and looked up at Bright, her eyes gone flinty. "Where's his mother?"

"She passed."

The auntly woman looked at Bright for a long moment and then back down at the boy. The younger one leaned in for a closer look at the baby. The children sucked on candies near the door or else fussed around an old tomcat suffering them from a patch of sun by the front window. "Margaret," the older woman asked, "will it be you or I that shows this poor man how to change a diaper?"

"You do it," the girl named Margaret said. "You're so much better at it than me."

The old woman shook her head in disapproval. "Well, if you haven't learned yet I just don't know . . ."

"Oh, I don't have to do any of *that* kind of thing," Margaret said. "They have their own nannies for *that* kind of thing."

The auntly woman shook her head again at this. She looked back up at Bright. "Are you coming from the fire?" It was the first time that Bright had heard someone besides the angel or himself speak of it.

"I saw it yesterday morning," he said finally.

They looked at him expectantly, waiting for more.

"After he was born and"—he paused—"and . . ." He looked at the box of matches there on the counter. "Yes, Ma'am, I saw it," he said.

"Mmm." The auntly woman's mouth set grimly, her eyes roaming over the naked baby. Then, drawing in her breath and pulling herself straight, she said, "Well, it'll be here by tomorrow

49

or the day after if the weather doesn't change." She looked around the store. "We had a fire here when I was a girl," she said. "Well, not here, but next town over. Anyhow, my father took the register out of the store with the help of three men, and they pulled it down the road on slats and buried it in our front yard. My father was a good man, always fair. Half the people in town saw him bury it there, but he knew it would be safe. The fire burned down the whole town, but he came back and dug up the cash register—this very cash register—and we started new right here."

"When did your wife die?" Margaret asked, interrupting the older woman.

"Margaret!" the older woman barked. "Keep your mouth shut, if you don't have any sense at all." She wiped the child's little legs clean with a rag.

"Day before yesterday," Bright said.

"Oh." Margaret looked down at the floorboards. "I'm sorry," she said. "What's your baby's name?"

"Margaret! Tell me I didn't just tell you to keep your mouth shut?"

"He doesn't have a name," Henry mumbled. He watched the auntly lady twist the ends of the diaper so that the whole assemblage seemed to wrap itself around his boy like magic. The spell of white fabric was held by two pins that materialized from the same nowhere that the diaper itself had.

"Well, you need a name for him," the auntly one said. "Have you thought maybe about naming him after yourself?"

"He don't need any kind of name like mine."

"What's that?" Margaret asked.

"Henry Bright."

"Well, what's wrong with a name like that?" Margaret asked. She turned to the auntly lady. "What's wrong with the name Henry, after all?"

"Not a thing," the auntly one replied. "What boy wouldn't be proud to carry his father's name? And a man like you who went to war and fought for his country?" She clucked her tongue and reached beneath the counter, pulling out a horsehair brush that she passed to the girl. "Margaret, reach up there and brush all that dust off his nice uniform. The shoulders there," she said, "and his back," she said, directing as the girl ran the soft brush over his uniform as she might dust a mantelpiece. "There." Margaret passed the brush back to her. "I'm giving you a drop of cinnamon oil here . . . and here." She put a dab of the warm-smelling stuff on either side of the sling hanging on his chest, then gave him back the boy. "Keeps the mosquitoes away," she winked. She stood back from the counter and looked at Bright. "And for you, I have some cheese and crackers. I don't like the looks of how thin you are in that uniform." She placed a large wedge of hard white cheese in a square of brown paper and laid a package of crackers alongside it.

There arose the sound of an automobile outside, and the girl Margaret looked back toward the door, where her brood was trying to teach the tomcat how to lick a stick of candy. "That's our car. I have to go now," she said. "Mr. Bright, I'm very sorry for your loss. Everyone!" She clapped her hands for their attention and the children piled out of the store.

"Learn to tie a diaper!" the auntly one yelled after her as the door closed.

12

The men spread out as they approached the church, their eyes roving over the village square for any danger that might lurk in the debris. Bright reached the immense doors first, and at a signal from the sergeant, the others spread to either side. The wood was stained almost to ebony by age, and the weighty brass rings that served as handles were polished yellow at their base from centuries of use.

They waited on Sergeant Carlson for the signal to open the heavy doors, and, when he gave it, they grabbed the rings and pulled hard until a small crack afforded Bright a look inside. The sanctuary was narrow, the floor a diamond-checkerboard pattern of slate and marble. The walls had been painted an austere white but were stippled here and there with muted flecks of color as daylight shone through the few remaining stained-glass windows, as through the prism of an icicle. An altar hunkered squatly on a dais at the far end of the room, one corner chipped away, a candlestick fallen to the floor.

Bright signaled that the room was empty, and at another sign from Carlson, he slipped inside. In the single, brief moment before the others crowded in around him, he let his eyes rise to the painted ceiling and, unprepared for what he saw there, found himself falling headlong into the crowded heaven that spiraled into infinity above him.

It was the blue of the sky that caught him first: a rapturous, painfully pure spike of color that hooked his eyes like fish and reeled them upward into the heights. Gone in that instant was the viscous puddle of October light that had dribbled in behind him through the crack in the doorway. Beneath the gracious blue vault of the church it was a fresh and dazzling spring morning at the beginning of the world.

His hand shot out, gripping the brass door handle hard, as if to keep himself from falling upward. He had believed the church to be empty, but, hanging there, Henry Bright realized he was in fact surrounded on all sides by a great gesticulating host of fellow beings. There were thousands of them in the sky around him—men, women, and children, in every conceivable pose and color. Some had the muscular builds of riverboat men and stood proudly astride their cake-white clouds. Others, a species of fat-faced-baby things, seemed to have leavened their way into the clouds themselves and popped their tousled heads at random from out of the billows, wearing expressions of frantic mirth and mischief. Many figures in the assemblage thrummed musical instruments, while others placidly displayed brutal and mysterious wounds. A finely featured woman held a pair of eyeballs on a platter, next to a nearly naked man who was calmly watching his own body being rendered into fat by flames.

Above this crowd and higher still, a circle of bearded and wild men looked down from their perches with electric severity at Henry Bright, though he barely noticed them. His eyes now had come to rest on the figure of a young girl kneeling in prayer there in the highest heavens at the dome's apogee.

She was almost impossibly beautiful, her eyes filled with such reserves of comfort that to Bright it seemed as if, had he come into the church only an instant earlier, she would have been happy to give him all the love and understanding he might have ever needed or desired. Sadly, though, this was not to be, for her face was even now caught in the act of turning toward the other figure who was interrupting her prayers.

This other interloper was an angel, its hair like twists of fire, its wings bejeweled with eyes in all states of opening and closing, its white robes trailing just behind it in this, its moment of arrival. It was impossible to tell what the angel was saying to the girl, but so beautiful was she, so composed and fatalistic was the poetry of her face against the urgency of the angel's, that Henry Bright fell in love with her in that moment and stood staring up at her as if stricken.

"Bright!"

"Bright?"

Bathing in the radiant pool of the girl's beauty, he was deaf to the men behind him and returned blinkingly to himself only to discover that he had been jostled forward by the others as they pushed past him into the church.

"Jesus! Would ya look at that!"

"Jesus my foot! Chaplain was right. Catholics. Nothing here but a bunch of dirty pictures. We oughta—"

The pealing bells above came back to him now and, turning, he found that he was standing before a small stone archway past which a staircase led upward into the bell tower. As the others argued with one another or else stood silently looking up into the blue, Bright stepped through the archway and began to climb the stairs.

13

Without his mother's rifle, and with little money left to buy provisions, the winter was very hard. The wind shrieked and the stream froze solid. He melted snow for water in which to boil the dwindling reserves of dried corn and bitter carrots. Rachel had terrible pains and sickness for a while. Her tongue turned a bright red and she ran a fever, but she didn't miscarry.

When the temperature dropped so low that the chickens stopped laying eggs, hc brought them inside and they lived with the clucking all hours. The goats dug for forage some, but as the snow got deeper all the animals got thinner. He killed the first kid and they ate the thing down to nothing. Rachel's health made an improvement. He killed another and made a stew with a few potatoes and the last of the carrots. She ate this for a week, and gradually the fever broke and her tongue returned to its normal shade. Now that they were inside the cabin, the hens began laying again. In the mornings there would be eggs in the folds of their blanket, in the bottom of the bucket, in the heel of a boot. She got up often now and would peek out at the horse through the freezing crack between the cabin flap and the door frame.

The horse was enduring the winter only slightly better than the goats. Its thick coat hung loosely over ribs, which showed as plainly as the bars on an empty prison. Except for the times when Bright would rouse it for his rare trips to town, its breaths came slow and deep, as if it was waiting to be revived by a kiss of spring breeze or the chirp of returning birds. Rachel often asked to bring it into the house, something that Bright forbade explicitly. He returned from Fells Corner once to find that she had led the animal inside their cabin anyhow, throwing their quilt over it and stoking the fire. It had been hell getting the stubborn thing out again, but he relented somewhat after this episode and tied the animal to the leeward side of the cabin, where it would be most out of the wind.

They ate the last kid in late February, when the world was at its coldest, and by early March he had butchered the billy. By then they had both developed a rank distaste for goat meat, and this last sacrifice to their hunger and the hunger of the unborn child was the worst. When he cooked it, the room had filled with gamy, clinging steam.

She milked the she-goat every day, though, and somehow, slowly, the world began to get warmer and the slant of the sun began to find their faces when they would leave the cabin and tramp through the melting snow to the hutch where he had resettled the chickens. The horse was moved back from the side of the cabin to its customary spot under the chestnut tree. The she-goat began to get fat again, and Bright suspected that she came down off her perch on top of the hen hutch in the night and foraged, when she could be sure that he would not come out and slaughter her as he had the rest of her family.

By May, his wife's belly was big and they were happy. At night he would hold her close and she would tell him wild stories that came from her own mind. She never talked about her father and brothers. It was as if since her rescue they had ceased to exist for her, and if that was so he saw no need to remind her of them or of the awful threats the old man had made as they turned their backs on him and rode away together. Sometimes he would tell her about the War, but when he did it was always about little things: the finding, once, of a lemon, or the unlikely discovery of a bottle of clear liquor standing untouched in an exploded bar, the thick white towels at the hotel where he had stayed in Paris during his leave from the front. He never told her about the church or the angel or Bert, and if he ever got too close to those things, he would stop mid-sentence. She, sensing something in him, would help him to steer his stories until the tension in his voice was gone and the pounding in his chest had slowed.

"And where were you then?"

"In Saint-Mihiel."

"That's a pretty name. San Maheel."

"Yeah. In a graveyard."

"In a graveyard? You were in a graveyard?"

"Yeah. And we were all on our hands and knees, and the one guy next to me, Ezra, he froze because he saw a gravestone with his last name on it."

"Really? What was his last name?" Her fingertips stroked at the thin hair on his chest.

"I don't remember what it was. Ezra Something-or-Other. He saw it and he just froze there, and all the rest of us, we crawled on and didn't see him. Then someone noticed he was gone so I went back to find him and he was still there, down on all fours, staring at that gravestone like it was telling him something he didn't want to forget." Bright looked up into the ceiling rafters. "I said 'Hey, Ezra, hey, hey,' but he wasn't listening to me, he was listening to the stone, so I reached over and I grabbed him and hauled him around in front of me so that I could get him going. After a bit I got him moving again. He was real young, younger than me. So we were crawling around the stones to join the others when a shell landed right next to me. It shattered another gravestone and there was rock everywhere. I got some in my eyes and I was coughing on dust and for a second I thought that I was dead, but the shell didn't explode."

"Why?"

"I don't know. I guess it was—" He broke off and she waited for him to continue. When he didn't, she helped him finish the story.

"It was because God saw you helping that man and he said, 'Hmm! I like that boy Henry! I'm gonna keep him safe.'" She laughed quietly and held him and kept laughing to herself until she fell asleep. It was a playful laugh that bubbled up around them like a spring of freshwater. Sometimes he thought it was actually the child laughing inside her. He would fall asleep to that music, and some nights he would escape his dreams.

14

He saw the horse caroming wildly about the small chamber as he rounded the final curve of the steeple staircase. Whoever had led the animal up these perilous spiral steps had finished cruelly by tying its tail to one of the ropes that rang the bells above. He stood still in the entrance of the room and allowed the horse to see him. More boots were coming up the stairs behind him. He waved a hand behind his back and the footsteps halted. The whites of the horse's eyes sliced at the air fearfully, its mouth was specked with foam at the corners. Bright stayed at the edge of the room and did not move, and eventually the animal began to quiet. It stamped uncertainly in a pile of dung, but its huffing slowed and it focused on him, watching for what he was going to do.

Bright moved slowly across the room toward it until he was close enough to reach out and rest his palm on the animal's twitching flank. The bells above had fallen silent as it had stopped moving and the rope tied to its tail slackened. The horse whinnied a few times, but Bright kept his hand where it was, and when he judged it finally calm enough, he ran his palm down the length of the shivering body until he was holding the slack of the belfry rope in his hand. He slipped the rifle off his shoulder and, holding it by the stock, sawed through the rope.

Above them in the belfry, the bells jangled loudly at their sudden release from the horse's tail. Hearing the dreaded things unexpectedly once more, the animal spooked clattering across the stone floor and hurtling in headlong panic past the men pressed against the staircase walls. From below them came a frantic whinny followed by a single shot as the horse reached the sanctuary.

Bert stood at the bottom of the stairs, the officer's pistol dangling loosely in his hand. The horse lay a few feet away, nearly dead, its tongue tasting the dusty marble of the floor, its eyes watching the heavens painted above them.

They all stood around it dumbly until Sergeant Carlson stepped forward and shot the horse in the head. The animal lay still. He looked down at it, rasping a hand across his face. "Well," he said, raising his eyes and looking around him at the others, "we're not leaving a dead horse in a church." He removed his helmet and ran a hand through his hair. There were the beginnings of a smile at the edges of his mouth. "Anyone see anyplace to get a drink in this town?" he asked. Then the smile disappeared and he stepped back to survey the problem of the dead horse. "I'm buying for anybody who's ever moved a dead horse before." Bert was still standing by the door, the gun swinging slightly back and forth like a pendulum.

"Bert," he said, but Bert's eyes were far off beneath his yellow hair, as if he were looking at reflections in the pooling blood there on the checkered slabs.

"Bert!" Carlson stepped between the boy and the dead horse. "If I *ever* see that Kraut gun of yours again, I'm going to kick your teeth in."

It took ten of them to push and drag the horse by its legs and neck across the blood-slicked marble floor. Finally they got it down the nave and from there pulled it bruisingly down the steps and out under the full ominous weight of the afternoon sky. Then there was nowhere else to drag it, and so they all straightened and looked around at one another and then around at the shattered village, unsure of what to do next.

Bright took off his helmet and walked back up the steps and into the church for a last look at the girl on the ceiling, but the light through the transept windows had begun to fade and he had to squint now to read her features. Then, hearing the sergeant call his name, he turned and walked out past the immense wooden doors to rejoin the company. He had just replaced his helmet when the air above them screamed and the church exploded.

15

Back in the sunlight, a sack of rag diapers in his arms, a new box of matches in his pocket, and his son clean and dry in the sling on his chest, Bright watched the girl named Margaret as she glided down the street above her throng of children.

"The Future King of Heaven needs that woman, Henry Bright."

Bright said nothing, tying the bundle of diapers to the saddle pommel, where they would hang next to the bucket of goat's milk.

"The Future King of Heaven needs a mother," the angel said again.

He untied the goat and then swung the animals around in the direction from which they'd come into town.

"She will suckle your child. Your son needs a mother or he will die. He will starve."

"He ain't gonna starve. I been feeding him, haven't I?"

"Your child cannot live long on goat milk. See how skinny he is. How slight."

Bright ignored the angel and began to lead the party up Main Street. Off in the distance the smoke from the fire painted the sky a sulfurous gray. The wind picked up, its hot tail whipping against their faces as it sucked past them.

"Bithiah," the angel began.

"You're talking nonsense and I don't want to hear it," Bright said as he watched the darkly spreading wings to the west. "Did you see that car? A girl like that, and all them kids dressed up so pretty, ribbons in their hair? Did you see her?" He coughed. "What would a girl like that need with my boy and me?"

"Bithiah," the angel continued, "was the daughter of the Pharaoh. She found a baby boy floating in a basket of reeds and she raised him as her own. This child was the prophet Moses. He grew up to lead the children of Israel out of Egypt."

"I know all that," Bright said. "My mother read that to me all the time when I was little."

"The Pharaoh's daughter was named Bithiah," the angel said again.

Bright pulled the animal up short. The goat continued on until it reached the end of its lead and came to a stop in the middle of the road. "I said I know all that," he said, exasperated.

"Her name is there in the Bible. Bithiah. You could look it up."

Bright scuffed the macadam with the sole of his boot and turned to look back down the street. Margaret was ushering the children into the big black auto. "Now you're just trying to make me mad," he said. "You know that it *ain't* her name we're arguing about. And," he added, "I *couldn't* look up her name if I wanted to, because you made me go and tear up the Bible to start the fire, remember?" He leaned toward the horse, waving his arm toward the wall of smoke. "Maybe you don't remember this, but my wife *just* died! Rachel? The one you liked so much? The one who gave you apples and corn?" His eyes were watering, and he spit to clear the catch from his voice. "You told me she was gonna be safe!" He gave the lead a jerk and got the animal moving again. It plodded stubbornly along behind him.

"The girl's many children need a father, Henry Bright.

63

When she approaches, you will tell her of the Future King of Heaven. The words will be put into your mouth."

Bright turned and saw the big black auto rolling slowly toward them on its way down the street. The car stopped a few yards away and waited for Bright and his animals to move out of its path.

"Do it now," the angel commanded. "The child must be fed. He must be taken in by a woman and cared for. He will surely die otherwise . . ."

For a moment the horse looked down its nose at the driver and the driver looked across the leather steering wheel and back at the horse. Bright wavered and then left his animals blocking the road and went to bend down level with Margaret's face in the back passenger window.

"I mean to say thank you for your treating Henry so good back there in the store."

The children were up on their knees in the wide backseat, giggling at the funny-looking horse and goat in the middle of the street.

She smiled. "Are you going to name him Henry?"

"I guess I am." She squinted at him against the sunlight, his mouth hanging part ways open as he waited for the words the angel had promised would be given to him. Then he closed it and turned to glare at the horse, but the animal seemed oblivious to his discomfort and continued staring down its nose at the car and its driver.

"Henry needs a mother," Bright said. "He . . . He's . . . an important child," he said. "He's to be important. I think."

He paused painfully again, and waited for any kind of help at all from the angel. "I'm a good man," he said. "Your children need a father."

He pinched the bridge of his nose between a thumb and forefinger and closed his eyes briefly in tribute to his own frus-

64

tration. "I mean," he said, opening them again and speaking more slowly, "I believe . . . that you and I . . . that maybe you and I could . . ." When the words didn't come he thrust a hand into his pocket, pulling out his mother's ancient ivory comb. He offered it to the girl through the car's window. "I'm sorry if this don't make much sense. My wife died two days ago."

Margaret turned in her seat to look at the children. They were watching the strange man and his animals in rapt fascination, as if a single sound might break the magic spell of their presence there in the middle of the road. The wind peppered stray bits of grit against Bright's face, and the goat began to snuff her nose at some message in the air. The lights in the girl's eyes did not dim but became sadder somehow. She looked at the comb in his outstretched hand and then gently placed her fingertips against his palm and pushed it back at him. "I'm sorry she died," Margaret said. She reached her hand through the window and brushed it against the child's copper-colored head in its sling. She smiled at him, a beautiful smile, like a dream in passing. Then the driver backed up and swung around them, leaving Henry Bright and his livestock to stand dumb, dirty, and still in the rising heat of the afternoon.

16

The concussive shock of the first shell hitting the church was the only one Bright actually felt. After that came the now-familiar feeling of capsized calm in which the world seemed viewed from beneath a great depth of water. It was as if all sound and feeling were gone suddenly, and, within that watery silence, death was not something hurtled from above but more like a meadow of wildflowers that blossomed from the ground in radii of plaster, mud, and dust, swallowing buildings and bodies, chewing them in the air a while and then spitting them back out upon the trammeled ground like the ends of gnawed bones. When the flowers finally stopped blossoming, the earth lay back down again and the senses returned.

After several minutes he began to pick his way through the church rubble in search of the others. Bert and Sergeant Carlson were the only ones that he found alive. Carlson lay next to an avalanche of roofing tile by the enormous splinter of the fallen steeple. He had a hole in his chest that had not yet begun to bleed but hung open in an "O" that looked like a mouth that was about to start screaming. He was breathing, but that was all. Bert was unhurt, though his pale face was pocked with plaster and his eyes were wide and shiny.

"That was really something, huh? Wow!" he said. "I mean, wow!"

Bright stooped next to Carlson. "Help me."

"You bet!" Bert said, but he didn't move. "How you doin', Sergeant? Don't you worry none, you hear me? You're doin' real good, real good!" He laughed to himself in disbelief. "Jee-roosh! We had a tight one today, didn't we, boys?" He was staring at the bodies scattered about; his brow was furrowing and unfurrowing. "Jee-roosh!" he said again. He began to shake.

"Help me," Bright said again, but Bert's whole body was now convulsing in some no-man's-land between laughter and sobs. Bright stood, hauled back, and hit Bert hard with the flat of his hand. "Help me," he said one last time, and Bert's eyes focused and he stopped shaking so much. "We need to move him someplace safe," Bright said. The sergeant's wound had finally begun to bleed.

It was terrible ground to try to carry a man over, and Carlson's feet shambled loosely against the pebble and debris as his legs began the process of forgetting how to walk. They passed the ruins of the church and had made it about a hundred yards down the road before Bright began to wonder if he'd been turned around by the shellings. Without the steeple it was hard to tell, suddenly, which direction they had first entered the village by. It was also beginning to get dark, and so he pulled Bert and the sergeant to the side of the road and down into a ditch by a stone wall. The hate had begun now, and stretching away for miles to either side of them came the sounds of the War.

Artillery passed high above their heads in singsong trajectories that merged and lifted with one another into strange musical chords, like cats crossing pump organs. The gigantic trench mortars were the loudest, the reverberations of their fusillades abating slowly across the night sky, briefly disappearing behind the sound of howitzers before the red-hot shards of metal they had fired into the air came screaming earthward once more.

"We'll go back to the line tonight," he said to Bert. "After dark." They angled Carlson into a sitting position against the wall and Bright put his ear close to the dying man. The sergeant's wound burbled as if a flock of sparrows had made a nest deep in his chest. To their left the road led back into the little town square and, to their right, sixty or seventy more yards down the road, hunched a glowering stone farmhouse.

"Why not take him over yonder?" Bert asked, motioning toward it.

"That's no good for us if someone comes in the night. They'll check the buildings first. We're better here." He looked down at Carlson.

"The hell we are!" Bert snapped. "And, anyway, like we got to be afraid of anything! You and I, we're good old West Virginia boys!" He pulled the German pistol from the waistband of his trousers. It was silver and shiny and seemed to distill, like dew, all the light from the darkening gray sky, so that the sky itself grew darker as Bert rolled the gun first one way and then another in his hands. Its barrel looked as narrow as a knitting needle. Bert pointed it at Bright an uncomfortable second, then laughed. "Boy, didn't I get you good?" He laughed again at the memory of frightening Bright with the gun as he'd come around the doorway of the deserted trench. "You 'bout shit your britches! You thought some big old Kraut had you dead by rights! Pow," he said, puffing the air.

Bright looked steadily at Bert and said nothing.

"I killed that Kraut officer," Bert said with petulance. "I know you all don't think that's so, but I did. He was gonna shoot me dead, but I shot him first." He turned it around so that the handle was to Bright. "And, look at this." He reached to light a match.

"No matches," Bright said.

"I want to show you the carvings and what all that's on the handle. They're something devilish. Dang! It's too dark to see 'em." He made again to strike a match. "Here."

"No matches. No light."

"Fine," Bert sighed. "Anyway, if you weren't so scared, you could see it's got a handle that's pure gold or something and carved with all that crazy Kraut writing. And if you'd let me strike a match, I was gonna show you the dragon with the spear through its neck. So don't you tell me that we got anything to worry about, 'cause if any Kraut Boche Fritzy decides he's gonna scout that farmhouse over yonder while we're in it, he's gonna find out exactly what the last fella found out who thought he could outdraw me." He tossed the gun in the air and caught it with surprising grace. "Now, Bright, let's get the sergeant over to that farmhouse and not say anything more about it."

"We're staying here."

Bert's face fell in the purpling light. "Is that all?" he whined. "Here we are, so close to those stinkers we can smell the pickles, and we're just going to hide out until we can sneak on back with our tails between our legs?" He poked the toe of Bright's boot with the pistol barrel. "Hell! This is as close as we're gonna get to them? What am I supposed to say when I get home? That I didn't kill a German the whole time I was in France?"

"I thought you did kill one."

Carlson coughed wetly then, expectorating blood. He raised his head and banged it against the wall several times like a man fluffing a pillow. There was a gravelly sound from his chest.

Bert looked at the dying sergeant a moment and then back at Bright. He stood up. "Boy, I know you want to, boy," he said to Bright as one might talk to a fire being stoked. "I know you want to go after them too! Ooooh, I can see it! I can see it in your eyes! You're a good old West Virginia boy!"

"All right," Bright said finally. "You want to go over to that farmhouse, go on over there. Check to make sure it's safe, and if it is, then we'll all go over. If it isn't, you just go ahead and kill as many Germans as you find in there." He tossed his canteen up at Bert. Bert stood looking at it. "Sergeant's thirsty too. You find any water, you bring plenty back for him." Bright handed him Carlson's canteen as well. "Well, go on," he said. "Git."

Bert looked from the empty canteens in his hands to the farmhouse waiting for him in the failing light. "Well, I ain't going over there alone," he said, and squatted back down again next to Bright. "And don't you go orderin' me to do nothin' either. We do things together."

"We can't leave him here alone," Bright said, nodding at Carlson. "And we can't carry him. And he needs water."

"You go, then," Bert said, and pushed the canteens back at Bright. He unhooked his own canteen and placed it atop the other two. "I'll wait here."

Bright peered through the darkness for signs of danger, but everything around him was a testament to that, so he climbed cautiously from the ditch and headed toward the farmhouse, crouching low as he hurried down the road with the empty canteens in his arms. He slowed as he approached the dwelling. The once-white paint gave off a muted glow against the fields, and the slate shingles were scruffy with lichen. The windowpanes were mostly gone from their frames, save for a few stray shards that glinted viciously out at him from the gloom like fangs. He went to his knees and peered between them into the dwelling, but it was as dark in there as a crack in the earth. He got to his feet and began to search for water. On the far side of the house he found what he was looking for. He held one of the canteens under the spigot but the pump handle dangled uselessly on its hinge. After a minute of pumping, he abandoned it for the stone livestock trough that his eyes now made out dimly, set flush against the house's wall. In the shadow of the farmhouse, the rainwater that came up to the lip of the cistern looked like a sheet of black glass. He knelt down in the mud and quietly set the empty canteens next to one another at his knees before lifting the first one above the still surface of the water.

"Wait."

At the sound of the voice, the world fell silent. There was no night breeze, no rifle fire. Even the large-caliber guns seemed to pause from their thundering and look around themselves, as if the unexpected word had wandered in like a small child and interrupted their supper conversation.

Bright stopped as well, the canteen in his hand frozen above the trough. It was impossible to tell how distant the voice was or even if it had been speaking to him. It had seemed to come from all directions at once, a calm command without emotion. He lifted his eyes to the farmhouse window above the trough, expecting to see a face framed in it peering out at him, but the darkness there was just as still and solid as it had been before. Beneath his hand, the water's obsidian surface reflected the shadow of the canteen against a cold backdrop of stars. He knew then that whoever was speaking must be behind him, training a rifle at the back of his head, a killer whose face he would never see.

"I . . . I'm fetching water," he stammered. "I got a shot man and I'm fetching him some water."

He took the silence that followed as incomprehension or consideration.

"English?" he asked. "American? Water?" He waited for an answer, thinking of the rifle slung on his back. There would be no time. He put his hands in the air, one still clutching the empty canteen, and stood slowly. "Water?" he said again, turning to face the man who had snuck up behind him. There was nothing and no one there. He shifted to the right and left, then made a full circle in the darkness to show whoever had whispered that he was only holding a canteen in his hand. "Water?" Running was hopeless, the voice had been too close. He waited for a reply another minute at least, but the hidden man did not answer. Expecting at any moment to be killed, he stooped to the trough once more and put the canteen to the surface of the water.

"Wait," the voice commanded.

He froze again. "Who are you?" he said, louder now. Compared to the hidden man's voice his own sounded thin and desperate.

A faint scent, insidious and sharp as chopped radishes, rose to his nostrils. In an instant he had thrown the canteen on the ground and dropped his hand to grope at the belt where he kept his gas mask. It wasn't there, and he searched frantically for it before realizing that he'd left it with his jacket back in the ditch by the stone wall. Cold panic held him for an instant, then drifted away like mist. He'd heard no shells fall nearby.

It was still possible he had missed the sound of a gas canister, which traveled at slower speeds than artillery shells and hummed lowly like old men in workshops as they flew. When a gas alarm was raised, you had six seconds to get your mask on or, if not, you had two days in which to experience annihilating agony and then forever to be either dead or terribly wounded. There were many false gas alarms on the line, and men were forever putting on and taking off their masks. Sometimes men would dream the alarm in their sleep and would open their eyes with their masks already on, having put them on without waking. Phosgene, if you noticed it at all, smelled of new-cut grass. The next day, however, you were coughing up pints of thick yellow fluid from your lungs every hour, and the day after that you were headed for a lifetime in some peeling hospital, the helpless ward of aging nurses. Unlike phosgene, mustard gas didn't even need to be inhaled. It was heavy, gangrenous stuff that trundled close to the ground, burning any skin that it came in contact with and causing huge, disfiguring blisters. Eventually the gas would settle, collecting with the rainwater in greasy floating slicks at the bottom of shell craters, potholes, and trenches.

His temples were throbbing and he realized that he had been holding his breath. He let it out slowly and sniffed the air again. The smell of the gas was certainly there but it was very faint. Looking down, his eyes came to rest on the trough. In the darkness, its pale-gray stone shone up around the water it held like the wide mouth of some monstrous fish. Whatever mustard gas had recently drifted through this farmyard was gone now, save for the stuff that had settled in a thin layer over the surface of the water in the trough.

All at once, with a kind of pent-up gaiety, the War started up once more where it had left off. In the distance, explosions strobed haphazardly against whatever poor clouds had wandered into the path of the big guns. Bright stared down into the gape of the great fish's mouth until he'd finally caught his breath and his heartbeat had slowed. Then he picked up the canteen from the ground and replaced its top before stooping to collect the others.

When he got back to the stone wall, Bert was asleep and Carlson was dead. He looked at the sergeant's face a long minute and then sat down again next to his remaining companion and waited.

It was well past midnight when Bright stood again and nudged Bert awake with his boot. He awoke violently, his pistol flashing out in the starlight. Bright knelt and put his hand against Bert's chest to hold him still. "Sergeant's dead."

"Yeah?"

"Time to go."

Bert leaned out over the ditch and looked up and down the

road. "So that's that?" he asked, his voice rising, turning harsher between his teeth. "We're just gonna run, huh?"

"We have to go before it starts to get light. If it gets to be morning and we're on the wrong side of the line, we'll be in worse trouble than we are now."

"We'll make a great sight then, won't we?" Bert jeered. He fumbled angrily in his pocket for a cigarette. "You may not have to impress anybody, but I gotta go and take over the bank, and what am I gonna say when some little old lady comes to my desk and asks me, 'Now, what was you doin' while the whole army got blown to pieces? Boy, you sure are lucky to have made it alive! And not a scratch! Land!' What am I gonna tell her, Bright? I ain't gonna say I sat in a ditch by the side of the road in the middle of the whole German army, am I?" He reached to light a cigarette. Bright pushed the match down once more.

"I told you, no fire."

"Fuck it, Bright. Fuck you." The match flared and Bert began to smoke his last cigarette. When he was half through, he turned toward Bright and said, "You know—" and was shot in the head from somewhere in the dark. Bright rolled over and flattened himself in the ditch, pulling Bert down on top of him. "Whew!" said Bert. "Jee-roosh!" he sighed. Finally he said, "Well," and that was the last he said of anything.

17

The car carrying Margaret and her children moved down Main Street, past the coal-company office and a church to where the trees took over and the large houses lulled in the shade of the overhanging elms. Bright watched it until it was gone, then he sagged in the heat. He recognized the kind of smile the girl Margaret had given him. It was the kind of smile that people give to children, and he surely knew what it meant when she gave it to him. Rising up from the sling on his chest now came the smell of his son dirtying his new diaper. He yanked a fresh rag from the sack hanging off the saddle pommel.

"You are a coward, Henry Bright."

"Goddamn it! Why you always got to talk to me when I'm covered in shit? You know I ain't a coward! And, anyways, why didn't you jump in and give me something to say when she was smiling at me like that?"

"Coward," the angel said again.

Bright spit on the ground. "You're a big one to talk," he said. "If you're so brave, why didn't you stay in France? You didn't go and find another church to go be an angel in because you were afraid of getting bombed again, weren't you? That's it, isn't it? You were scared just like everyone else."

"The Future King of Heaven needs his swaddling changed."

"I'm getting to that, so be quiet, 'cause I'm talking now." Bright whipped the white rag in the air before the horse's face. "What about when I needed you on the field after I got shot? Where were you then? You were hiding is what. Scared is what you were! You're the coward, not me." He shook his head as he knelt and spread his jacket on the hot pavement, then laid the new diaper on the jacket.

"Henry Bright, you are so blinded with fear that you refuse to see that I am trying to help you now, just as I helped you then."

"How are you trying to help me?" Bright took his son from the sling and rested him gently on the jacket. As he waited for an answer, he began hesitatingly to tie the new diaper as the auntly woman had taught him to do in the store. "Exactly how you're helping is what I don't know," he said again, looking up once from where he knelt near the horse's hooves.

"I am trying, despite all your best efforts to the contrary, to find you a mother for your son, the Future King of Heaven. As I was telling you before you allowed the girl Margaret to escape, the boy needs a woman who will claim him as her own. You cannot care for him by yourself. Now we must follow her. She must take the boy or all is surely lost."

"What do you care if he's safe anyhow, angel? You weren't so careful with me when I got shot in the War. I lay there for hours and called for you, but you didn't come. And you didn't care any when Rachel was dying either, did you? She was screaming—*screaming!*—and you didn't care. You just stood out there under that chestnut tree like you were asleep."

"You survived. I knew that you would. And Rachel lived long enough to fulfill her destiny as the mother of Jee-roosh. I never assured you of her well-being past that point."

"What's that supposed to mean?"

76

"What's what supposed to mean?"

"Jee-roosh?" Bright replaced his son in the sling. The baby cooed up at him. "What are you saying 'Jee-roosh' for?"

"The time has come to name the child. He shall be named Jee-roosh."

"No, it ain't!" Bright said. "Oh, no, it ain't, angel." He climbed into the saddle. "He's my son and his name is going to be Henry, like me." The angel said nothing, as the horse's big jaws worked a cud. "And Henry's a good name too, angel," Bright continued. "You have a problem with a name like that?" Its ears twitched and it lifted its tail, allowing several large balls of dung to fall to the pavement.

Bright sat up in the saddle. "That's real polite," he said. He gave the horse a sharp kick with his heels to get it moving.

"Very well," the horse said. It swished the argument away with its tail and began to clomp along in the direction that Margaret's car had gone. They passed a group of men loitering around the coal-company office. "For now the Future King of Heaven's name is Henry, but it will be Jee-roosh as the boy grows older, and men will speak the name with awe as the centuries unfold. Your own name will be recalled from time to time."

They went by the church and the spreading elms and through the smell of green onions and pecan pie, roasting chicken, and garden laughter, through the dark mahogany sound of someone playing hymns on a piano and the far-off thrumming of a train. The breeze had dropped as they walked up the street, but now it picked up again, the leaves above beginning to clap against one another as the air blew warmer. The goat, normally so quick to dart this way and that on her tether, now stayed close to the horse and lifted her white nose again to snuff at the black scrolls of smoke garlanding the air.

"Smoke's getting a lot stronger," Bright said.

"Yes."

"Fire's gonna burn this place down."

"It would seem so."

The road passed the last of the big white homes and swished through a series of lazy bends as the smell of smoke grew first stronger, then weaker, and then stronger again in the uncertain breeze. Bright let the reins hang loosely in his hand, allowing the horse to slouch unhurriedly down the middle of the road until at last they pulled to a halt before a gigantic gate, its ornate wings swung wide. The road continued on, bisecting a rolling ocean of tight green grass, threading its way between several nickel-colored ponds and curling itself finally around a gushing fountain. Behind the fountain, like a series of new white molars, rose a huge and beautiful palace. Margaret's auto was parked there at the foot of a set of creamy steps that led up to the gleaming golden front door.

"The girl Margaret waits within. Go to her quickly."

"That place ain't hers," Bright said, shaking his head.

"Think again, Henry Bright."

"Even if it was hers, if you think I'm impressed by a palace you can forget it," Bright said. "I seen a hundred palaces in France, all of them just like this one here." His eyes drifted across the expanse of green to the building a long moment.

The wind buffeted again at their backs, as if to push him forward, but before he took a step the driver of Margaret's car emerged from the palace, carrying the bags for a finely dressed couple and a young child. He ushered them into the auto, then arranged their luggage on the car's roof before getting in behind the wheel and circling around the fountain and back down the road, toward the gate where Bright now stood. His path once more blocked by Bright and his animals, the driver slowed to a crawl and stopped until Bright pulled the livestock to the side of the road and let the car pass. As it did, Bright recognized the child within as one from the clutch that had surrounded Margaret earlier. She was a little girl with a wine-colored cap, and she now sat happily on the lap of a woman who was clearly her mother.

"Well," Bright said, turning to face the horse.

"Go to Margaret, Henry Bright."

"She ain't no mother of five children, you idiot! She probably ain't even a mother at all." He swung his arm behind in the direction of the palace. "And that palace over there? That's a hotel! I seen those in France too. I even stayed in one once. Either you're trying to trick me or you don't know what you're talking about."

"I am only trying to help you."

"Some help you are. That girl Margaret minds children for rich folks." He threw a caustic laugh in the horse's face. A touch of spittle landed on the its dark nose, startling the beast. *"You know everything!* I just bet you do!"

The angel was silent.

Bright tied the horse's lead tightly around a tree. Then he went to fill a pail with water from one of the small ponds on the lawn. He came back into the trees and plunked the bucket down in front of the horse. "Everything you told me so far has been wrong," he said, as it lowered its head to drink. "I come back from the War and you show up all of a sudden, tell me I gotta go steal Rachel from her own house, and I listen to you and go on over there and get her in the middle of the night and the old man comes out yelling he's gonna kill me. Then she's having a baby and you don't help us and she dies. Rachel! Now the Colonel and his boys are gonna kill me and take my son—"

"The old man and the half-wits are not chasing you," the angel interrupted.

"You say that, but you been wrong about everything else!"

"They are not chasing you."

79

"I loved Rachel, angel! I loved her! Maybe you don't know about that kind of thing."

"You are being a coward, Henry Bright. Go and—"

"She was my wife!" he screamed. His eyes were red-rimmed and welled with tears. His lower lip trembled. There was a twitch in the skin over his cheekbone and he tried to smooth it out by rasping a hand over his face and looking up into the hazy sky until he had composed himself. "And *now*," he said, once he was able to continue, "you want me to give my boy to that girl Margaret in there because you say she's a mother, and now I find out that she's not even a mother at all."

The goat began to pull on its tether, straining toward a bush. Bright bent and untied it to forage. The horse rumbled deep in its throat.

"You'll get your food when I say you do," he snapped. "And I'll tell you another thing: Everything you tell me is wrong and makes me look like a fool. So why am I supposed to believe you? And don't say something like, 'It's because I know,' 'cause we both know that ain't gonna wash with me no more." He took the baby out of its sling and laid it on his jacket on the ground.

"Go."

"No, no, no! I ain't going. This is a wild-goose chase. Only thing we got to do is stay away from the Colonel, and that's just what we're gonna do. We'll stop here tonight and head out in the morning. We'll ride another piece tomorrow and another piece the next day."

"The boy will die."

"He ain't gonna die. I ain't gonna let him die, but I ain't gonna do everything you say anymore just 'cause you tell me to." He threw himself on the ground next to his son and cast one arm over his eyes. "If you want that girl so much, then *you* should go and ask her to be *your* mother. We'll just leave you behind in the morning, see if we don't." He rolled over. "Go to hell."

He lay there for a while, and the horse held its peace. Eventually Bright got up, emptied the bucket of water, and went to pick the goat up and carry it out of the dark-green leaves where it was munching contentedly. He milked it for a bit, then set up camp and ate the crackers and wedge of cheese that the woman had given him at the general-merchandise store. After a little while, the big black auto came back, empty of its passengers and their bags. The birds began to sing and then they stopped, and the sky began to darken as night fell. Finally the moon rose, nearly full, but its light seemed to be shining down through a trough of smoke-slicked water, and across the lawn the white hotel fell into dark shadow beneath stars that were fainter than they should have been.

18

Henry's mother taught him how to take care of the rabbits and chickens that they kept in a hutch near the chestnut tree. In the late summer the two of them would eat apples and then push the cores through the fencing and sit watching as the two species shared the remainders decorously with one another. In the mornings the hens liked to lay their eggs in the warmth where the rabbits had been sleeping, and they would squabble and squawk the rabbits out of their beds. This always made his mother laugh, no matter how many times she saw it, and when he heard her laugh it would make Henry laugh too.

The garden patch would be thick with vegetables, and when she gave him haircuts she would keep his hair and show him how to tie it up into little bundles which they would hang on the fence posts around the garden to keep the deer away from the vegetables. He would pick runner beans and bring them to her, and she would put them in jars and boil the jars and then put them on the shelf for winter. When they could get to the tomatoes before the birds did, they would preserve those too, but not before they ate some with eggs and bread.

They had summer squash and acorn squash and some stalks of corn. She would make the corn silk into a beard and hold it to her face like a monster and chase him around with it while he screamed in terrified delight and the chickens and rabbits clacked and scampered in their pen.

When he was seven and it was time for him to start going to school in Fells Corner, she got a job cooking for an old couple in town. Each morning, after the chickens and rabbits had been fed, they would head out. Whatever else she took with her, his mother always carried her rifle slung across her shoulders, and he knew to be quiet and not talk while they passed the turnoff to the Colonel's house. She would grip his hand hard then, pulling him along, so that he could never see past the first bend in the drive. He knew somehow that she had used to live there, until something bad had happened.

When the Colonel's little boys, Corwin and Duncan, started to come to school too, sometimes they would all be on the road together at the same time. He knew his mother didn't like them, was maybe even afraid of them the way she was always sure to place herself between them and Henry as they walked.

Sometimes it was the Colonel's little girl, Rachel, who would be standing at the end of the drive of his mother's old house, waiting for them to walk by so that she could join them. His mother liked Rachel. She was a funny one, his mother said. She would tell funny stories about big green monsters and beautiful ladies and knights that lived in castles and chased wild pigs. And she was pretty, his mother said. Her clothes were very bad, though. Her skirts were muddy at the hems, and even the parts that weren't muddy were dirty, like they had never been washed. She never had any food with her and she smelled bad. Her hair was all knotted, and she had a single green ribbon that she always untied from her hair and tied round her wrist because she liked to see it and was afraid to lose it. Even the ribbon was dirty, though.

One time, while he and Rachel were walking ahead of his mother, Rachel made him hold her hand and told him that they were going to get married. He didn't say anything. It was like she had cast a special spell for him, like the women in the stories she told. He didn't want to ruin her spell. Even after the teacher told Corwin and Duncan that they couldn't come to school anymore, for the way they were with the other children, Rachel still came each morning, walking alongside Henry and his mother. His mother put more food in Henry's lunch bucket. She began to bring the beautiful ivory comb with her, and with it she would work the knots out of the girl's hair before they came in view of the schoolhouse.

For the Christmas program, Henry was to be a donkey and Rachel was to be an angel. His mother made him funny brown ears from the fabric of a flour sack and they practiced making donkey sounds for weeks. On the night of the program, they crunched through the snow and met Rachel in the darkness at the end of her drive, and then they all walked together. When they got to the schoolhouse, it was brightly lit and whole sleighloads of people were arriving in their best clothes. Before they went in, Henry's mother tied a new piece of ribbon—bright and glossy gold—around the girl's head.

"There, you beautiful girl," she had said. "Now you look like a real angel with your own halo."

Even from the vantage point of a donkey, Rachel had looked glorious.

Henry was eight years old before he saw the Colonel. He came to their cabin on the very day that the first green blades of corn began knifing through the slush of the farmyard. He had gray hair cut close. His beard was trim and the same color of gray as the hair at his temples. His eyes were flat and spoon-colored, set within an angular face that seemed carved out of a large block of salt. His back, beneath a military uniform much frayed from use, was so straight and sharp of shoulder, and his legs in their black riding boots so thin and knobble-kneed, that the man seemed almost to have been fashioned in a workshop rather than a womb. To Henry, he looked like the monster his mother pretended to be sometimes when she would hold the corn silk to her face and chase him around the yard. Henry knew then that the man was the Colonel, and that the Colonel was a monster too. He waited for Henry to fetch his mother.

When she came, she stood at the cabin flap and looked at the Colonel for a long moment. She put her hands on Henry's shoulders and pulled the boy closer to her. "What can we help you with today, sir?" she said. "Maybe you'll want some tomatoes or some beans and then you'll go on your way." She did not ask the man inside.

"She is dying," the Colonel said. "She has been calling for you."

His mother's tongue caught in her throat with a click until she forcibly cleared it. She let go of Henry's shoulders and wiped her hands on her apron at the words. "All right." She disappeared into the blackness of the cabin, and when she reappeared her hair was tied back and she was no longer wearing the apron. Her knuckles knotted and unknotted themselves around the stock of the rifle that she held between her breasts. "This is loaded," she told the Colonel. Then, to Henry, "Henry, wash your face and fetch a clean shirt. Quick, now, we're going to meet your aunt Rebecca."

Henry did as he was told and came to stand by his mother and the Colonel.

"Good man." The Colonel smiled faintly down at him. "Rum rations doubled." He bowed and swept a courtly arm up the road.

"Don't speak to my son," his mother said. "And we'll walk behind you, not the other way around."

"Chivalry is—"

"Keep it," she said.

As they came up the drive, Henry was happy to see Rachel standing on the porch, but when they got closer he could see that she had been crying. His mother saw the girl too, and she slung the rifle by its strap over her back. It rattled against her shoulder blades as she ran up the steps and pulled the girl close. Only when she saw the Colonel's two boys standing silently in the open door did she become wary once more and release Rachel, pulling the gun back around into her hands so that the barrel pointed at the space of porch between her own feet and the boys'. Corwin, thick-lipped, his eyes cast downward and his fingers kneading themselves into fat fists, refused to acknowledge Henry or Henry's mother. Duncan, yowl-eyed and willowy, regarded them both with the steadiness of an underfed barn cat. Henry's mother turned to the Colonel. "Where is she?"

Henry followed her through the front door and into the gloom of the Colonel's house. In front of them a staircase led to the second floor, but his mother did not ascend it, instead veering left and into a large sitting room festooned with portraits. Here the air was heavy and the light pierced through the gaptoothed slats of the shutters like hot knitting needles. A woman dressed in an old gown lay on her back upon a table in the middle of the room. Henry's mother went to the head of the table and gazed down. That the women were sisters was unmistakable, and yet, while Henry's mother was healthy and strong, her sister's face was sunken, her arms at her sides like sticks, her tiny feet laced tightly within ankle-high black boots. She did not seem able to move save for her eyes, which blinked at a crack in the ceiling plaster above her.

"Colonel," his mother said, as she turned and fixed the man with a look of hatred, "I'll ask you for a few minutes alone with

86

my sister please." The Colonel backed out of the archway, through the front door and down to the yard. When he was gone, she turned and leaned over the woman. "Rebecca?" She said the name very quietly. "Rebecca? Can you hear me?" She laid her hand on the table and then rested it on her sister's hand. "He came and told me you were asking for me." She beckoned Henry to her side. "Henry, come here and say hello to your aunt Rebecca."

Henry had been standing in the center of the room, afraid of the woman on the table in front of him, and afraid of Corwin and Duncan standing with Rachel in the archway behind. He approached slowly. The woman tore her eyes off the ceiling crack and looked at Henry blisteringly. Her pupils were very large in the dimness and they jittered back and forth like birds in shaken cages. He had to look away, and when he looked back her eyes were once more fastened on the ceiling above.

"Last time you saw him was when he was born," his mother said. "He's growing up into a big strong man like our own brother Henry was." The woman's hands were small and seemed covered over with the kind of thin, beautiful skin that frogs have. "It's all right about everything," his mother said to the woman. "I know it didn't turn out like you thought it would. It didn't turn out that way for me either. We both know where things went wrong, but it's no good worrying about any of it now. The world got us all at once. First with our Henry dying in the Philippines, then Mother and Father"—here she turned and looked out the window at the Colonel on the lawn—"then my own husband buried in the coal mine before he could lay eyes on his son." She raised Rebecca's hands a little and then lowered them again as she leaned over her. "Too much," she said quietly. "Too much all at once." She let go of the woman's hands in order to fasten a stray button at the top of the woman's neckline. "We can't blame each other for all the things we said to each other that we didn't mean, but I know we can't say we're sorry either. So I'll just say that I love you. I love you so much. Looks like you have some really fine children here, and I'm gonna pray for them. I'm gonna pray really hard for them and I'm gonna pray hard for you and that we meet again in a better world than this one we've been given." She bent and kissed her sister on each of her cheeks and then, taking the ivory comb from the folds of her skirt, she began to comb the woman's hair. "I'm not gonna leave you here like this," she said, her voice turning as thin and jagged as the crack in the ceiling.

"Children," she said. "If you stay, you need to bow your heads and close your eyes and don't open them again, no matter what you do, until I tell you that you can. Henry, go on over there with Rachel and the boys and bow your head too." They did as they were told and she began, her back to them and standing over her sister. "Heavenly Father, if it is true that you give us sorrow and joy in equal measure according to the strength of our backs to bear the load, have mercy on your daughter Rebecca and give her now the joy in her new life that you withheld from her in this one." Henry opened his eyes to peek at his mother, but he couldn't see her face. "We pray that as she enters your kingdom . . ."

Her voice left off suddenly and her body hunched with some strange effort, her head bowed from sight beneath the line of her shoulders. The rifle slung over his mother's shoulder shifted this way and that as if it was aiming at some high-flying, far-off bird. Rebecca's tiny boots kicked against the table three or four times, then lay still.

In the silence that followed, Henry looked over at Rachel and her brothers. Corwin and Rachel's heads were bowed, but Duncan's eyes were wide open and he was watching Henry's mother as well. After a long while a sigh escaped her lips and she continued, "We pray, Heavenly Father, that as she enters your kingdom you will offer her some explanation for the sorrows that you, in your infinite wisdom, saw fit to visit upon her." His mother's hands dropped to her sides all at once. She turned, the rifle butt clanking hard against the parquet as she sank to the floor. She pulled the gun around and laid it across her lap, leaning back against one of the table legs for support. She closed her eyes. "Amen."

She opened them again. Her hair was mussed, her face as waxen as her dead sister's. Corwin and Rachel still had their eyes closed and their heads bowed. She glanced at Henry and then at Duncan. The boy looked back at her steadily. She looked more exhausted than Henry had ever seen her. She reached behind with one hand and used the lip of the table to pull herself to standing. "Corwin, Rachel, you can open your eyes now. Henry," she said, "come along with me."

She walked through the upper rooms, standing in doorways, trailing her hands absentmindedly behind her along the walls as if her fingertips were collecting old memories. Here and there a few strips of dirty wallpaper had once been printed with lilac bunches and roses. One room had been a nursery, and where there had been a water closet, part of the wall had fallen away, the room dropping off abruptly into open air and the dusty lawn below. The tub and washbasin were filled with old charcoal.

There was a sharp, mildewed odor to the rooms. Plaster pieces lay fallen and cracked everywhere. One room was bare save for a pair of boots lined up against a wall, a broomstick planted stick-down in the hole of one as if awaiting the firing squad. "It didn't used to look like this, Henry," she blurted all at once, standing framed in the crumbling hallway. "It was a beautiful house once. Do you believe me?"

89

He went to take her hand, but she brushed by him now and ran down the stairs. He went to a window and looked down to the yard where she had joined the Colonel. She was leaning forward and speaking to the man's unmoving profile, strands of her hair escaping the knot she had tied it in and puffing into cirri around her face. Henry crept down the stairs to the porch and stood half hidden in the doorway, next to Rachel. The Colonel seemed oblivious to his mother's ferocious presence. He stared off into nothing as she spat words so quietly at him that Henry couldn't make them out.

Just when it seemed he had turned into some Civil War statue the Colonel collapsed from his reverie and walked to the squash patch and pulled a rusty shovel from where it was stuck into the ground. "Boys!" he yelled toward the house, and looked off into the far distance as he waited for an answer. When none came, he did not call again, instead holding the shovel handle toward the open doorway where Henry was standing.

Henry's mother snatched it away from the Colonel and stepped back, the shovel in one tightly clenched hand, the rifle in the other. "What in God's name *are* you?" she hissed. "Henry!"

He was down off the porch and at her side in a moment. She did not look away from the Colonel as she held the rifle down for him to hold. "You remember how to use this, don't you?"

Henry nodded, taking the gun in his hands.

"Yes, you do. And you remember how I taught you to pull the hammer back so the gun is cocked and ready to fire?"

He nodded his head once more.

"Good," she said. "Now, I want you to cock the gun carefully, all right? Pull it back with your thumb like I showed you." There was a click as the hammer locked. "Good, Henry." She seemed to exhale forever. "Now I want you to point it at him, and if you see him move from where he's standing, I want you to shoot him dead." Her eyes flitted quickly down to see if he'd comprehended. "Do you understand me? If he moves while I'm digging this hole, I want you to shoot him dead in the face. You don't even ask me if you should; you just pull the trigger. I need you to protect me, Henry. Can you do that?"

He clenched the rifle so tightly in his hands that his fingers began to tingle and whiten. In answer, he pointed the gun up at the Colonel's head. The Colonel stared hard at Henry, and those spoon-colored eyes frightened him, but he hid the man's face behind the eclipse of the rifle barrel and kept it there as his mother dug the grave.

The early-spring ground was still frozen solid beneath the slush, and digging was nearly impossible. She chiseled away at it nevertheless, steam rising first from her mouth and then from her entire body before she broke down and sat in the middle of the shallow gash she had cut in the yard. When she caught her breath she got up and began again. Henry's arms began to tire and his fingers to feel numb from holding the heavy rifle trained on the Colonel. By the time his mother had dug a trench two and a half feet deep he was nearly weeping from the weight of the thing. She stood back and let the shovel fall on the frozen pile of chipped dirt by the side of the hole. She came and knelt next to Henry. He tried to give the rifle to her but after an hour his fingers seemed locked around it. Her eyes shone as she eased the hammer back down and helped each of his fingers to uncurl from the gun. "That was just fine, Henry. Your father would be proud of you." She kissed his cheek and then heaved herself up with the rifle and walked up the steps into the house. The Colonel followed close behind her.

Standing at the foot of the table, she took her sister's ankles in her blistered hands and made ready to lift them. The

Colonel went to the head and stood looking down into his wife's face. He removed his broad-brimmed hat and ran his hand through the plastered strands of his hair. "Well, that is that," he said. He reset his hat firmly on his head and strode from the room without a second glance, leaving her still holding the dead woman's ankles at the foot of the table.

She set the legs down and came to kneel next to Henry. "I'm going to need your help one more time. This will be hard, but we'll go slowly. Will that be all right?"

Henry looked out the doorway where the Colonel had gone and nodded yes.

"Now, I want you to go to where I was standing and I want you to try to hold those legs up while I pull her off the table. Can you do that?"

He nodded again and went to where she had been standing.

His mother took the body by the armpits and began to pull it slowly down the length of the table. Henry followed the dead woman's feet as they slid down the long plane of wood, and he tried to catch them as his mother finally pulled the last length of the woman's body off the table, but the legs were too heavy and the little black boots passed through his hands and thumped to the floor. His mother caught her breath and considered her sister's body. She looked at the doorway warily before taking the rifle from around her back and nestling it in her sister's arms. They half carried, half dragged the deadweight a few feet at a time until, as they passed into the hallway and neared the front door, his mother gave up trying to carry the body at all. Instead, she grabbed whole ripping handfuls of the woman's gown and heaved her over the threshold and down the porch stairs each step punctuated by the dragging *rat-tat* thump of the boots. At last the body rested in the dirt at the Colonel's feet. She bent and pulled the rifle from her sister's embrace.

"You haven't got a box, have you?"

The Colonel stood erect and did not reply, so she cocked the rifle and handed it back to Henry, who pointed it at the man while she climbed into the shallow grave and pulled the body in after her.

She took a long time arranging her sister in the narrow hole, brushing the dust as best she could off the gown, combing her hair once more with the ivory comb. The arms, which had twisted in their joints from being dragged, did not look right. She tucked them behind the body, so that the dead woman appeared to be clasping her hands behind her as she walked through a doorway from one world into the next.

Finally, she closed her sister's eyes, climbed out of the grave, and, after taking the rifle back from Henry, allowed her gaze to rove the house and the overgrown craze of bramble and crabgrass that lived in its shadow. She put a hand on Henry's shoulder. "We're going now," she said to the Colonel. "She was my sister but she was your wife, and I'll not be the one to bury her. That's for you to do, and I know you know how to do that at least," she said. "It didn't take you long to get my father in the ground. If he'd known what kind of a man you really were, he'd have shot you down like a sick horse. He might not have been a colonel, like you claimed to be, but he fought in a war too, and when he came home he held his head high." She spat on the ground. "Look at you," she said to the uniformed figure, "*Colonel* Morse." She said the name as if it were a bad taste. "They were all so proud of you. She was so proud of you. A colonel. The last man to know my brother." She snorted once with derisive finality. "To think anyone was ever worried about the family name because I married a coal miner."

The Colonel's eyes raked across her face, but he said nothing.

"Rachel," she said to the small girl in the doorway. "I want you to come live with Henry and me now. Just leave your things and come along. This isn't the place for you to live anymore."

"Leave her be," the Colonel said quietly. "That is my daughter."

The girl in the threshold curled her neck around the door frame like a little swan, her body still subsumed by the interior shadows behind her.

Henry's mother raised the rifle with one hand until it was pointing at the Colonel. With the other hand she beckoned to the girl. "Rachel? Just come along now, all right? You're going to come and live with us."

The girl wavered, looking in confusion between the face of Henry's mother and the Colonel. The man did not turn to his daughter but continued to regard Henry's mother.

"It's all right, girl," his mother said. "He isn't gonna hurt you. He knows this is no place for little girls. You know that too, don't you? Come along now."

The girl's dirty face flickered. She unfolded herself from the door frame and came walking slowly down off the porch. The Colonel lunged and grabbed her as she was about to pass. He pulled her close to him, and the girl did not resist, appeared in fact to relax into the surety of her father's grip.

"She is my daughter," the Colonel said. "You dare insult a grieving man."

"Rachel," Henry's mother said. "Little girl, if you ever need anything, if anything ever happens to you, I want you to come find me, do you hear? You know where we live."

All the way back to the cabin, his mother walked facing backward, the rifle gripped so hard in her hands that her knuckles looked as if they might pop out from beneath her skin. Once they were home, she put it up in the rafters where she always kept it and sat down on the footstool by the empty fireplace a long, long time, rubbing her shins beneath her skirt and staring into the charred rocks at the bottom of the flue. Henry went outside and played with the rabbits and chickens through the fencing. As the sun was going down, he went and threw rocks on the road. Only when the sky was as black as the fireplace itself did his mother emerge from the cabin and fetch some wood for a cook fire.

19

The night passed with agonizing slowness as Bright lay in the ditch beneath Bert's body. He thought for a long time about the girl in the church, about her beautiful face and the way that she had looked down from the ceiling at him in the very instant he had put his head through the doorway. It had been as if, in that moment, the girl had wished to go with him but knew that she never could, that her fatc was elsewhere. He knew that look well. He'd seen it on Rachel's face the last time she had come to their house.

It had been almost two weeks since the death of his aunt Rebecca, and his own mother had been in the house working to mend a hole in the bed quilt. Henry had been in the yard when he glanced up and saw the girl standing there in the road. He knew immediately that everything was different now. She was not the same girl that he had been walking to school with every morning for two years, not the same one who had told him that he and she would one day be married or who had laughingly piled the peeping golden chicks on his chest. This girl looked as if some giant from one of her own stories had stooped down and whispered the world's largest, worst secrets in her ear. She was barefoot. He could have gone to her, but something, some new kind of law, prevented it. Instead, he had raised his hand to her and she, after a moment, returned the gesture. The golden ribbon was tied around her wrist. She had looked at Henry with the same expression on her face as the girl on the church ceiling. It was a look of farewell, he realized now, lying there in the ditch. She had come to tell him goodbye. She never went to school or came back to the cabin again after that day. Perhaps she didn't even remember who he was anymore.

"She does."

The world once again got very still, very small at the sound of the voice.

"You hear me, Henry Bright." The voice was very close to his ear in the blackness.

"Yes," he said finally. Then, "Who are you?"

"I am an angel, Henry Bright, be not afraid."

"I am." His throat was tight with fear and the words came out with a cracked, whistling sound. "I am afraid."

"Be not," the voice said again.

"Where are you?"

"Henry Bright, be quiet. Look."

He was quiet and he looked. The sky was getting infinitesimally lighter now, and in the farmhouse down the road, through the gaping holes of one of the window frames, he saw something move. It was slight, a kind of rustle upon the eyes that carried no sound, but it was there nonetheless. "Who is it?"

"I am an angel. Be not afraid."

"No," he whispered. "Who is that down there, moving around down there?"

"You must lie very still."

The squat figure of a stoop-shouldered man emerged from the house. He stood there in the door frame and looked up into the blue moonlit sky before walking into the middle of the road and stretching, as if just having risen from a heavy meal. The doorway disgorged another figure, this one much thinner than his companion. The two stood in confab a moment, the silver splinters of rifle barrels glinting down their backs in the moonlight. It was too dark to tell what uniforms they wore, but as the duo began to walk down the road in his direction, their movements were animated with a kind of easy contentment, as if whichever side they belonged to, they felt quite safe in their surroundings.

He tried to pull Bert's body even farther on top of him.

"Lie still, Henry Bright."

He lay still as they passed him by, but they could not have gone twenty feet when Bert's empty canteen shifted somehow in the dark and fell against the stone wall, making a clinking sound. Bright caught his breath and, as he did, Bert's corpse shifted above him once again, the dead man's head lolling to release a stream of cold, thick fluid onto his face. He coughed quietly once against the wetness.

"Lie still, Henry Bright."

The footsteps pulled up short and stood there in silence. Then the boots came back, mulching and sucking against the mud of the road.

"Close your eyes. Do it now."

He closed his eyes and pretended to be dead. The boots stood there in the darkness a long time. Then there came a cracking of joints and the crunkle of leather as one of the figures stooped to a squat for a closer look. A hand came down softly on Bert's back, resting there like the kind of close friend that it was likely Bert had never had. The hand whispered up and down the fabric of the dead man's back two or three times and then a palm was running along the scalp of Bert's head, and more cold fluid dripped and slid onto Bright's face. The fingers trailed down past Bert's ear and then down the nape of the dead man's neck until they came to rest on the crest of Bright's eyebrow. He held his breath in agony as the hand made its way across the wet, sticky surface of his eyelids, down his cheek, and then slowly pried his lips apart and slid into his mouth. The fingers worked between Bright's teeth and under his tongue as he struggled to hold his breath. Just when he felt that he might explode from lack of air, the fingers pulled away and the figure stood. A metallic sound was followed by a quick punch of pressure from above, and a harsh, sulfurous rip of air escaped Bert's bloating body through the puncture made by a bayonet. The blade came down hard three more times, but due to Bert's girth Bright was untouched. What followed was the kind of long, steady silence that accompanies surveyal, and Bright waited behind closed eyes for the bayonet to come for him, but the awful silence went on for so long that he began to wonder whether the figures had somehow slipped away. When the agony of waiting was too much for him, he found himself, almost against his own volition, opening his eyes a fraction in the moonlight, catching the men's familiar faces in the instant before they turned and continued walking away from him down the road. He did not need an angel to tell him who it was he had seen.

20

Bright couldn't sleep, and so he lay looking at the bilious sky and the hotel, which sat in its pool of electric light there in the middle of the darkened lawn. On occasion the breeze scooped up a few jostling strains of music being played on a piano, and once or twice voices broke out in singing. The infuriating horse shifted lazily on its feet but then slept. It lay down once to dream, but then it got up again. When the baby cried he fed it from the goat's milk and rocked it slowly until it fell asleep again. Later, he woke to find the hotel silent, and he changed the boy's diaper in the darkness. When this was done, he fed it once more. Rachel's nipples had been small, thimbly things, much tinier than his big index finger. On impulse, he dipped his little finger in the milk and offered it to his son. The boy took it in his mouth and suckled greedily.

She had been out milking the goat when her water broke. As usual in warm summer weather, she was naked, the skin stretched tightly across her enormous belly. She stood there in the yard and called to him. The goat was standing near the puddle of fluid, neck craned up at her. Together the goat and the girl looked at Bright. He had tried to pick her up to take her inside, but she had waved him away and finished milking the goat first.

He stood above her, unsure of whether to touch her or not,

and then after a while he went to stand with the horse under the chestnut tree. "Well," he said, "I guess that it's happening now. This is what we talked about, ain't it?" He watched the girl milk. The horse was not watching, but its nostrils flared, pulling in drafts of the new scent and chuffing them out again. "And she's happy, ain't she? I mean, we're going to have a baby. What I mean to say is, thank you for making me go over there and steal her away."

The horse said nothing in reply.

"Angel?" he said, but if the angel was there it gave no answer.

His wife stood then, the bucket in her hand. "Maybe it's time we went in to the bed and see what happens," she said, and held an arm out for him to slip his shoulder under.

He went to her then, the angel forgotten, and carried her feetfirst through the cabin flap, one arm holding the bucket, one arm slung around his neck.

That was the last time she ever put her arm around him. After that had come a feverish nightmare that he could remember only pieces of. The baby's head was large, and he had twisted around sideways. Bright had been forced to reach in, as he'd seen a man do once with a cow, and pull the infant out by its heels. At some point during this time Rachel had died. He wasn't sure quite when. Maybe she had looked at him and tried to say something. Maybe she had said something. She could have been screaming something; he might have been screaming too, but suddenly there was only a single sound in the cabin, and that was the crying of their son, the boy who now lay in a clean diaper against his chest.

21

They had watched the young boys as they fished and played in the swimming hole below the railroad trestle. When the sun was starting to sink, the Colonel and his sons emerged from the trees and made themselves known to the boys, who looked at the Colonel in his tattered uniform as if he were some kind of Confederate ghost. While Corwin and Duncan stood on the bank, the Colonel waded into the middle of the stream up to his waist and stiffly saluted the boys on the far bank.

"Which of you here is the eldest?" he called out to them.

The narrow-chested boy who had examined Bright's uniform lifted his hand. He was perhaps ten years old.

"I see," the Colonel said with a curt nod. "And did you take any part in the recent War?"

The boy was baffled and looked at his friends for some kind of answer to the strange man's question.

"You mean over there?" another boy said.

"That is correct, sir," the Colonel replied. "Over there."

"No," the boy said. He puffed out his chest. "But I woulda gone!"

"Brave boy, brave boy," the Colonel said quietly, as the

stream rushed around him. "Of that I have no doubt. You may observe that I also am a soldier."

The boy nodded.

"A soldier always recognizes a brother soldier. It has nothing to do with uniform. It has to do with bearing." He leaned forward in the flow and lowered his voice conspiratorially. "My own sons, the ones on the far bank back there, are not soldiers, sadly. They have none of your martial bearing."

"We saw another soldier here today," the boy said.

"Yes?"

"Yessir."

"Good man. That was my next question. He must have been my son-in-law. A great war hero."

"A war hero?"

"Oh, yes. And did he have a child with him?"

"Yessir. He had a little baby, and a white goat that climbs on rocks, and a horse too."

"A little baby, did you say?"

"Yessir."

"We were escaping the fire and were separated in the confusion. Can you tell me which way he went?"

Corwin and Duncan had begun to set up camp when he waded back across the stream. "The rogue made his way to a town not far from here. He is bent on some new seduction, no doubt. Probably already visiting whores."

Duncan looked up from a pile of sticks that he was gathering together to build a fire.

"No doubt," Corwin said. "He's probably visiting whole bunches of 'em!"

"Contractions," the Colonel said.

"What?"

"I will not have sons of mine speaking in contractions," the

Colonel said very calmly. "'Ain't,' 'dasn't,' 'won't,' 'of 'em'—how many times have I berated you, beaten you both, in the vain hope that you will learn to speak in a manner that does not insult the listener with your ignorance?"

"Lots of times," Duncan said.

"What was that, my boy?"

"Lots of times," Duncan said again. "You've berated and beaten us lots of times."

The Colonel sighed and sat down in his wet boots and trousers. Almost immediately he stood up again.

"We will not sleep here tonight."

Corwin, who had found a patch of blackberries by the bank, looked up pleadingly. "Why not?"

"Because Henry Bright may come back in the night and find us unawares. Also, the fire is coming quite close. Should you prefer death by flames or rogue to a restful night's sleep, you are under no obligation to follow me to my mountainous redoubt."

"So?" Corwin gripped a blackberry bramble to pull himself up the bank and winced as the thorns cut into his hand. "So what if he comes? We'll kill that son of a whore, won't we?"

The Colonel threw a stick at Corwin. "Contractions! And, anyway," he lowered his voice, "how would you propose to kill Henry Bright, who has recently returned from the War and is well practiced in the taking of life?"

"We could shoot him with the rifle?"

"With the rifle? You may remember, my son, how, without permission, you went to shoot with the rifle in the woods, bringing it home to me without ammunition?"

Corwin looked down into the stream. "The knife, then?"

"Ah, yes, the knife." The Colonel took the blade out from his belt and held it up. "It *is* a fine blade. At any rate, I will sleep up there tonight." He turned and began walking toward the slope of tailings that led up the steep incline to the mouth of the tunnel.

Duncan stood and looked down blankly at the tinder he had carefully arranged for a fire. He ran a hand through his hair two or three times, then followed his father and brother.

"I bet he was visiting whole bunches of whores!" Corwin whispered again to Duncan after night had fallen and they were safely encamped in the railroad tunnel. "Whole bunches!" Duncan listened to his brother's conjectures without reply. "Whooooooooo!" Corwin hoot-owled behind him in the dark. "Ooooooooooo!" his echo came back.

"Silence!" the Colonel yelled. He lit his pipe with an ember from the fire and listened to the river below. "Mark me well, boys, Henry Bright is not content to seduce and murder only one woman; no, he will do it over and over again. He must be killed and his child taken and raised properly." He talked on like this for a little while, caught up in whores and murder.

At some point in his father's monologue and his brother's hooting, Duncan stepped from the mouth of the tunnel and climbed out onto an outcrop of the cliff face just to the side of the trestle tracks. He curved his thin torso tightly against the rock wall. "Train," he said softly.

It happened very fast. The light of the train filled the tunnel, and the breeze sucked past them; the Colonel left off from his sacred vows and bloody imaginings, and Corwin from his hooting. Both burst out of the tunnel's mouth and onto the moonlit trestle. Corwin found the opposite ledge from Duncan and somehow managed to pull his big body up onto it, hugging the cliff side in terror and leaving his father to stand blinded and trapped on the tracks above the abyss. The Colonel stood agape only a moment before he ripped his belt off. The knife fell away and was swallowed up by the emptiness. For an instant his

moving through every pocket and then searching his helmet before looking around in a mute panic at the others as they made their preparations. He had lost the address of a girl that he'd met on leave. Where could it be? Would he ever see her again? It was not a thing to worry about for a boy going almost certainly to death, but there it was, and what it was, it was. Another time, while sitting out a mortar barrage in a muddy, melting trench for almost six hours, Bright watched a man pour a portion of kerosene on a sleeping friend's foot and light the man's big toe on fire. The joke had been far more absorbing to everyone than the hell going on above.

Perhaps it was Bert who had chosen to speak Henry Bright's name as his last words, Bert who had somehow proclaimed himself an angel and warned him of the coming of the Colonel's sons. There were certainly stranger last words in the history of war. But what of the voice he had heard by the animal trough, the one that had told him to wait before dipping his canteen in the poisoned water? Could that voice really have been Bert's as well? There were no answers in that vacant stare. He relaxed his arms and let the body fall back on top of him.

Suddenly he heard voices coming toward him down the road. They were plain, real voices and, most important, they were discussing a Brooklyn Robins baseball game. "American!" he called out, but his voice was far gone from thirst and exhaustion, and it was hard to draw enough breath to yell with Bert's deadweight pressing down on his chest. "American," he said again, more softly.

A long, narrow face came into his vision. "Jesus! Nice place to go lie down! Give me a hand with the big one here," the slight man said to an apple-cheeked, larger man over his shoulder. The two rolled Bert's body off Bright. "They get you?"

"No." He lay there pressed into the mud of the ditch until they pulled him to his feet.

"What happened? Christ, look at your face."

Bright tried to wipe Bert's blood from his face with his jacket sleeve, but it had dried there and his lips were tacky with the stuff. He explained about the shelling of the village, leaving out the parts about the Colonel's sons and the angel's visitation.

The narrow-faced one looked at his bigger companion and they both burst out laughing. "Do you know how lucky you are, kid?" the narrow-faced one asked. "Krauts were only sixty yards away." He shifted a water bucket to his other hand and pointed with his free arm toward the farmhouse. "You slept next to 'em most of the night."

"How many were there?"

"Who knows, but they were busy."

"When did you get here?"

"We got orders to scout the village and find out what happened to you guys about an hour ago. Everyone was dead. Not a soul."

"'Cept you," the other one said.

"I saw them leave. There was only two of them."

"Bullshit."

"They came out of that house and walked right by here, then one came back and did that." He pointed down at the bloodless bayonet holes in Bert's back.

"Well, however many of 'em there were, there were enough," the shorter one said. "Take my word for it." He pointed over at the farmhouse one more time. "Or don't. Take a look in there and see for yourself."

They turned to continue walking, and Bright reached down to Bert's body and pulled the beautiful silver and gold pistol from where it was tucked in the waistband of the dead man's trousers. In the fresh morning light the gun looked sylvan, magical. The writing on the filigreed handle was in German and he could not read it, but the bullets—coppery nocturnal things asleep in their snug chambers—he understood well. He released the gate and emptied them onto the ground by the bodies of Bert and Carlson, then he followed the two men to a water pump that had been found in the square. They waited for Bright while he drank and washed Bert's blood from his face, then they went to stand joking by a group of ashen-faced others while Bright walked back down the road to the farmhouse from which he'd seen Duncan and Corwin emerge. The forced laughter of the men in the square followed him, a kind of despairing jollity that faded abruptly from his ears as he stooped to step inside the doorway. A chaplain was within, also gray in the face. He looked at Bright pleadingly and then spread his arms as if trying to encompass the pitiable carnage he stood in the midst of.

After she had waved goodbye to Henry, Rachel didn't come to meet him and his mother at the end of the drive for the walk to school anymore. They waited for her the first couple of days, but when she didn't come they kept going. His mother began to grip Henry's hand protectively for the first time in a long while. He was eight now and he didn't like that, but he let her do it anyway, because he knew she was scared.

One day after school he went to meet his mother where she cooked for the elderly couple in town, and the two of them had walked toward home, his mother's rifle, as ever, over her shoulder. As they neared the turn up to her old house, she gripped Henry's hand even harder than usual. "Hello, Duncan," she said. The boy was standing at the mouth of the drive, his head and thin body swaying slightly like a pitcher plant in the stillness. Although the weather was cool and he was still a boy, his sweat-soaked shirt clung to his chest and there were dark circles under his arms. Duncan said nothing in reply, but he repaid the stare Henry's mother gave him with his own implacable gaze, his thoughts as opaque as his pupils. Henry heard the rifle creak as she shifted it on her back. "Face forward, Henry," she said. "Chin up. Don't look back."

When they arrived home, they found the chickens dead in a white feathery pile, their necks broken. The rabbits had been killed as well and were now tied in drooping clusters to the fence posts around the garden, fastened with the twine that his mother had used to make bundles of Henry's hair. A few of the rabbits had been skinned, and these lay like enormous overripe strawberries in the middle of the garden, beneath where a stick had been stabbed into the ground. At the stick's top was tied the golden ribbon that his mother had given to Rachel at Christmas.

Bright backed out of the farmhouse and sank to his knees in the middle of the road. He vomited thinly, waited, then fell to all fours and gagged until his chest hurt and the sweat ran out of his scalp, down his face, and onto the ground. When he felt strong enough, he got to his feet and walked back to the town square to stand near the body of the dead horse that he had helped to drag from the church the day before. Fragments of plaster painted as blue as the sky itself lay scattered about. The next morning he was back in a cold, wet trench and November was beginning.

23

After he fell back asleep at the edge of the hotel lawn, Bright dreamed strange, feverish dreams. In one, he found himself rolling Duncan, still a young boy, over and over again in the muck of a field. In that strange currency of dreams, he found the boy to be weightless and his body spun in the mud like a log floating in a river. Each time the boy's face resurfaced, it was frozen in some new expression, sometimes smirking mischievously, sometimes grinning widely or pulled forcefully downward like a carp's yaw. Despite the ever-changing set of the mouth, however, the eyes were always empty black holes that bored fiercely into Bright. He became wildly angry. He began to kick and kick Duncan in the head, to no effect. He smelled the mustard gas, a tingling around his nostrils and lips punctuated by sharp little bites, as if he was about to be devoured by a swarm of insects. In his rage he could not stop kicking Duncan. The burning settled like bees around his mouth, and was followed quickly by an awful pain across his neck and chest; still, he could not stop kicking. Only when he knew that it was too late and that he would soon die of the gas did his anger begin to fold. Then he was simply staring at the thin little body bobbing in the muck. Duncan's eyes pulled him downward, and his awful grin had settled itself into a warm, welcoming smile.

Bright he awoke to the sounds of his son crying and the smell of smoke strong in his nose. It was far too early to be dawn, but the sky had taken on a diseased half-light. He propped himself on an elbow and made clucking sounds to comfort the child, but it continued to wail so loudly that Bright replaced the fragile bundle carefully on the blanket and reached for the bucket. He dipped his little finger in the milk for the boy to suckle, but the child was utterly wild in the darkness. He again went to hold his son close, but the boy's shit was everywhere and there was something frantic to the smell: a sour, unwholesome odor that rose from the child like heat. Bright got on his knees above the infant and struck a match; then, as if burned by what he saw, he fell backward. The match went out. In the gloom he put his fist to his mouth and bit down hard, a small sound escaping from far back in his throat. Sweat was running down his back in skeins. He lit another match and looked again. The child's face was covered in amber blisters the size and shape of pumpkin seeds; its mouth was a welter of pain.

He scurried backward on all fours into a thicket of brambles, tearing the skin of his hands and legs. He scratched the ground, clawing at the dirt in his confusion, aware of neither the piercing thorns nor the burning red wings that had spread themselves across his own face and chest while he slept. He looked up a moment at the sleeping horse, then hurriedly scooped the crazed child into his arms, broke out of the woods, and ran across the darkened lawn toward the hotel.

24

"Henry Bright."

He was digging a new latrine pit fifty yards distant from a row of Red Cross tents. If the voice startled him, he gave no indication and said nothing.

"Henry Bright."

A group of soldiers moved down the road—an exchange of shifts. The relievers were tense and quiet, the relieved looking drawn but laughing loudly as they walked.

"Henry Bright."

"I know who you are," he said at last. "You're the angel from the church." He made again to dig. His shovel had run up against the sodden wool of a buried uniform. There was no telling, with the muck, whose side it belonged to. He gave up trying to cut through it with the shovel blade and bent to pull it out with his hands. The ground sucked back hard and would not budge.

"Yes," said the angel. "Fear not."

"The big one talking to the girl up on the ceiling."

"Yes."

"I knew it was you. Why are you here?"

"Because now I'm talking to you."

He gave another great pull on the sleeve of the buried uniform, the veins on his forehead popping and his face going red with the effort. The jacket came away all at once in his hands and he fell backward against the side of the hole. He rested a moment there, and then threw the heavy mass on the ground before taking up the shovel again. He spoke under his breath, his eyes fixed on the latrine he was digging. "Why did you tell me to be quiet?"

"Because I wished to save your life. I have chosen you, Henry Bright. I saw what you tried to do for the horse in the church. I saw you looking up at us, the girl and me."

"Why are you here now?" he repeated. There was a tooth in the shovelful of dirt.

"The church was destroyed. I needed a place to go. I chose you and I am with you now."

"Was it you told me not to drink the water?"

"The water was poisoned," the angel said. "Mustard gas."

"Is it only you come from that church?"

"Yes."

"Where's the girl then? The one on the ceiling up there with you."

"The girl is gone. You and I will find a new girl."

"I'm just digging a latrine is all I'm doing," Bright said, but to whom he was speaking would have been obvious to no one.

115

25

Standing naked and willow-kneed there near the hotel fountain, he began to scream along with his child. Whoever woke
from sleep to peer down from the hundreds of windows at the
disturbance below saw a man who could just as easily have been
a ghost. His mouth hung open in a wail, and his silhouette, par-
tially obscured by the darkness of the drive, flickered with an
otherworldly translucence in the light cast by the corona of the
burning ridge behind him.

A light came on, and then another and another. Men dressed
in pajamas or hastily thrown-on shirts surrounded him with
their lanterns and loud voices. Tears and spittle ran down his
face. He held his son out at arm's length toward the uncertain
circle of men, as if blindly searching for an altar upon which to
offer up the tiny gargoyle of pain.

And then, parting it all, a small and round female figure in a
white apron stepped through the circle. Her hair was pulled
back and her face was indistinct, lit dimly as it was by the murky
orange sky, the lanterns, and the lights of the awoken hotel.
The woman approached Bright and his baby slowly.

"Now," she said. "Now, it's all right, it's all right." She talked
to him as if he were a shied horse and held out her arms to ac-

cept the child. "Give the baby to me." For a brief flash he thought that it was the girl Margaret, but even in his panic he realized that this woman was different, moved with greater bearing than the girl he had first followed to the hotel. She held his face in her gaze for a moment. Then, with what could only be a supernatural grace, she lifted the boy from his arms. The child pressed itself against her, almost butting at her chest with its head. Bright just stood there, his red-rimmed eyes blinking hard against the brightness of the lanterns. Then his teeth began to chatter and he seemed to discover his own nakedness and the red welts that had capered across his thin white chest. The woman put a hand to his head, still rocking the child, then she addressed the men within the circle of light.

"It's all right, gentlemen, just put down the lights, put down the lights, except for you, Dennis." A tall, sandy-haired man in work boots rubbed sleep from his eyes. "The rest of you, it's all right now, it's all right. Just go on back up to bed." She clucked down at Bright's son in her arms.

"You're going to let these two in the building?" a man asked. He had a burgundy nightshirt on, and he pulled incredulously on a corner of his mustache. "They might have the flu." He stepped forward and thrust his light in Bright's face. "Just look!" Bright shrank away from the sudden brilliance of the lantern, and the woman stepped between him and the man.

"I'll take the responsibility for these two myself," she said. The boy had begun to wail again, but his eyes were cried out. "We have a doctor on call in town. We'll send for him"—she turned to a young man groggily buttoning a tan and red uniform—"unless there's one staying here. Is there a doctor staying with us? Yes? Well, then, please wake and fetch him. Apologize, of course." She turned back to the men. "There. He's gone to fetch the doctor. I'll watch them in the meantime."

117

She looked at the man who had lunged at Bright with the lantern. "And you needn't fear; this isn't the first time someone wandered into a patch of poison ivy."

The men put out their lights, and the glow of the forest fire on the ridge seemed to grow brighter. "By the looks of things, I don't imagine that we'll all be worrying too much about poison ivy soon anyhow," she said. The group turned silently and looked at the flames. "Now, Dennis, help me get these two indoors. Sorry for the disturbance, gentlemen. See you in a few hours at breakfast." She carried the child to a set of steps leading down to a door that stood open in the foundation. Dennis followed her, helping Henry Bright to walk across the gravel drive and down the cool flags of the basement steps. The rest of the men stood in the drive by the fountain and stared at the approaching fire for a long time, the crying child and its raging father forgotten.

Bright was laid in a small bed in an empty white room. He cried out. The light burned his eyes.

The woman came in and placed wet rags on his face. "I've had a cradle brought down to my room," she said. "I'll look after your son until you're feeling a bit better, all right?"

Then he lay there, a sliver of yellow coming in from the hallway, and fell asleep as voices murmured low and soft next door. He woke once more in the night and something was poured down his throat. After that he slept, and if he dreamed, the dream was forgotten.

26

"Check his pockets."

"I know to check his pockets!" Bright was on burial detail.

"In his pockets there is a packet of cigarettes and a lemon."

"I know that already, 'cause I saw him put the lemon in his pocket! You saw me see him put the lemon in his pocket!"

"This one has no flask. That last one had a flask. It was in his boot."

"What do you need any whiskey for?"

"You could still get it. It's still there."

"How do you know?"

"I know everything, Henry Bright."

Henry Bright bent down and reached in the dead man's pocket to retrieve the lemon. Unlike the man, the lemon had escaped the machine guns unscathed. He put it into his own pocket and then began to roll the body slowly into the forty-foot-long hole that he and the others had dug for the bodies.

"The packet of cigarettes."

"Would you—" Bright swiped at his face in frustration; his voice dropped to a hiss between his teeth. "Would you just *stop* talking? I know all about the cigarettes and I was about to get them, but you're always, *always* talking at me. Can you *please* just be *quiet?*"

For a moment there was silence.

"Give the cigarettes to Sergeant Matthews."

Sergeant Matthews was his new sergeant, now that Carlson was dead back by the farmhouse near the village. He found Sergeant Matthews digging through another dead man's clothes, putting whatever he found into his own bulging pockets before rolling the body into the hole and standing up. He saluted the corpses. "Hinky, dinky, parley voo," he said. "*Adios*, so long, *adieu*."

"Sergeant. I thought you might want these." He held the cigarettes toward Sergeant Matthews with solemnity.

"Toss 'em here, Bright. There's a good kid." He lit one of the cigarettes and scoped, squinty-eyed, through the tobacco smoke at Bright. "You need to shave, Bright. You look like a German or a bomb-throwing anarchist." He looked down the line of bodies. There were thirty-six of them. "Or a German anarchist!" he erupted. He laughed for a little while about this. "Hmmmm," he said. Then he smoked the rest of the cigarette. "Well," he said. His eyes were red.

They were taking their time. The brigade had been sent into the woods on information that only the southernmost part of it was held by the enemy, and loosely at that. In reality, machine-gun emplacements were everywhere, and maybe six hundred men had been killed or wounded in the few minutes after the first companies had entered the forest. The advance had been a complete disaster, and the order to fall back came after one endless hour of slaughter. After that it had been two days of sitting in the mud, during which there had been much talk of the supposed armistice. Some said it would happen any day now, that the order would come and they would all rise from their trenches like the dead hearing the last trumpet sound, and head to Paris and eat steak with oyster mushrooms. Others had it on good authority that peace of any kind was as far away as the moon. Regardless of all conjecture, there followed a day and then another day of shells raining blindly into the trees as the enemy slowly relinquished ground. During this time the angel hadn't talked to Bright, though he had called for it several times. Now Bright and ten others were on burial duty. At first they had moved in pairs, picking up soldier after soldier by the boots and arms and placing them on the lip of the grave, but then time and the sloshing mess of it all began to eat away at the last vestiges of formality, and the men began to break from one another so that they could do the numbing job as quickly as possible. There were regulations about the respect to be shown toward American dead, but the numbers were enormous, and in the end the only concession that seemed to matter was that the bodies were rolled, not thrown, into their graves. The rules said nothing about what was supposed to happen to whatever money, chocolate, or cigarettes they might find while doing so.

"You find any lemons, Bright?"

"No."

"Huh. Well." Sergeant Matthews walked upwind of the grave with a few other men in the burial detail and stood there smoking.

Bright touched the lemon in his pocket. He smelled his fingers, smelled them again, and then rolled another man into the hole.

There came a short, sharp whistle, and a tremendous explosion threw Bright sidelong into the brush at the bottom of a tree trunk. After a while he woke up and blinked dozily. Above him in the sky, even the sun seemed to have been jostled from its slow transit by the force of the shell's impact. His ears were bleeding and a boot was resting against his cheek. He shrugged it off. It wasn't his. On the hillside around him, a few of the others raised their heads. He stood and picked up the leg, which he had buried ten minutes before, and tossed it back into the hole that they had almost finished filling when the shell hit. He and the others looked briefly for Sergeant Matthews and the other smoking men, finding only pieces here and there on the trees and scattered about the ground. These also were placed in the grave and covered.

He walked a hundred fifty yards back and lay down on his woolen blanket. His head was angled downhill, but he was too exhausted to change position. There was a mark on his face where the boot had kicked it. He took the lemon from his pocket. It was a small, runty thing with mottled skin. He put it to his nose and inhaled convulsively. Lifting it again above his face to look at it, he turned it over and over between his fingertips before finally putting it to his teeth. He bit a small hole in the rind and began to squeeze the fruit in his fist, gently, as one would milk an animal, coaxing the juice into his mouth. While he slowly pumped the lemon, his eyes turned themselves upward into the blank sky.

"What wreckage this King has wrought."

Bright took the lemon away and spoke softly. "Not now."

"A new King must be found. This one has soaked the world in blood. He has allowed War to become so terrible that it can kill all of mankind. No King of Heaven has ever allowed War to become so powerful."

"I said not now," Bright said again, and continued to suck the diminishing lemon until it was a leathery husk. Then he lay there, licking his teeth, contorting his lips as the sour taste turned somehow to sweetness on his tongue.

27

Light seeped in beneath the moist rags on his face, and he was being scooped up and carried in someone's arms. At first he knew it was the angel. Then he knew for sure that he was about to be rolled into a grave. He began to twist and kick out against the walls of a narrow hallway.

"Shh shh shh. It's all right," a woman's voice came cooing from nearby. "We're moving you someplace you can be more comfortable. Just lie still, lie still."

The arms held him close and he lay still.

They ascended a set of bare wooden stairs and went through a doorway, then the sound of the footsteps changed and they were clicking across stone. The rags fell from his eyes and he was looking into the face of the sandy-haired man who was carrying him, then past the man's face and up into a dome of painted blue sky. The ceiling was gently illuminated from below, as if the sun were about to rise in all directions. Aside from the chance embroidery of clouds, the sky was clear. There were no cherubs, no judges, no dying saints. There were no angels or mustard gas, no smoke or beautiful young girls; the dome was simply, blessedly, empty. He felt that he might like to drift in that sky forever, breathe that clean, cold air, and leave the earth below to consume itself.

They passed by a grand piano, a row of potted ferns lining the curvature of the wall, and finally out from under the dome and into a tight brass elevator. The doors closed and they moved upward. A cool hand rested against his head. "You have a fever," a woman's voice said. "I'm going to put these back over your eyes now."

He closed his eyes and felt the cool rags against his eyelids. The elevator chimed open and he was carried down a quiet hallway. There came a click as a door opened and then he was being laid on cool sheets.

"Thank you, Dennis," the woman said. A moment later the door clicked once more as the man who had carried him left the room.

"Water," Bright whispered. She helped him sit up and the rags fell away again, and he saw her distinctly for the first time. She was about the same age that he was: perhaps twenty, perhaps younger. Her face, like the rest of her, still had the soft glow of baby fat. There was a light-brown birthmark, like the silhouette of a duck's head, between her temple and her hairline. Her eyes were downcast.

"Where's my son?" he said after he had sipped from the glass she held to his lips. His voice was torn. "Where's my boy?"

She placed the glass on the nightstand and crossed the room to where a bowl had been set. "I'm keeping him in my room for the time being," she said quietly. "The doctor has been in to see him. His rash is worse than yours, but we rubbed him with jewelweed. He didn't like that very much, but he'll be all right." Their eyes met, and both looked away. "The doctor," she said. "The doctor gave me some salve and told me to put it on you." She paused a moment, embarrassed. "On your chest."

Bright said nothing and she came to the side of the bed to stand over him. Whatever was in the bowl was pasty and grayish in the low light. She pulled the sheet down slowly, exposing the amber blisters of the rash. "Oh," she said, and bit her lower lip.

"I dreamed that it was mustard gas," he said.

"What?"

"They would put the ones who got gassed in the same tents with everyone who got shot and shelled. The people who got shot didn't make much sound, just lay there feeling bad. The ones who got gassed, though, they cried all the time. Calling out. The nurses would set their sheets up like tents so no one would have to see them like that, but you could still hear them."

She took a dollop of the lotion on three fingers and held it suspended over his chest.

"Go on," he said to her. "Put it on."

"I'm sorry," she said again. She looked into his eyes briefly and then stared at his chest.

"They ain't gas burns," he said. "It won't be as bad as all that."

Still biting her lip, she daubed the cold poultice on the slight cavity below his sternum. He made a low rasp in the back of his throat and craned his neck backward against the pillow. She spread the lotion thickly over the welts and boils. "He said it was poison ivy, the doctor did. But he also said you were just worn out and needed to rest and eat." Her hands were so red and rough that, if it weren't for their size, they could have belonged to a man twice her age.

"I fetched my goat out of some bushes after it was dark. Must have been then. And then I went and fed my boy." He took a deep breath, winced, and let it out through his nose. "I about killed my own boy," he said. His head seemed to sink deeper into the pillow.

"It's not your fault." She took a rag and wiped her hands of the lotion, then began to wash them in the little marble sink. "It's not," she said. "Is that how you were feeding him? With the goat? Where is your wife?"

"She died," he said. He began to push himself up against the headboard. "Then there was the fire."

"It's coming close," the woman said. "Today is going to be a full day. Please lie down." She dried her hands on a towel and lightly pushed him back down with a few fingers on his shoulder.

"My horse and my goat need food and water," he said, staring upward at the white plaster ceiling with its fine cornice and moldings. "I need to go and fetch them."

"Dennis can go."

She began to move about the beautiful room, arranging some flowers in a vase on the mantel, fluffing the pillows, making sure the curtains were drawn tightly against the light. "Was your wife named Angel?" she asked.

"No." He looked at her suspiciously. "Why?"

"I'm sorry." She reddened, brushing a strand of hair behind her ear as she backed toward the bedroom door. "You were crying out in your sleep. I think that Angel is a beautiful name." She put her hand on the doorknob. "I'm very sorry I asked," she said again quietly. She opened the door and turned to leave.

"My name is Henry," he said. "Thank you for taking care of my boy and me."

"Mine is Brigid," she said. "I help to cook here." She switched off the lights. "It's still early. You should sleep more."

"I want to see my boy," he said, out of the curtained darkness.

"I'll bring him in to you once you've had a chance to rest a few more hours. Now sleep." She closed the door behind her, and Bright lay in the room's stately, cool gloom, a delicate floral smell like lavender rising from the medicine that she had rubbed on his chest.

28

The armistice that would end the War was to be signed at eleven in the morning. All fighting was to cease after that. Still, the hate came and went as usual at dawn, and, as the sun began to rise on the last day of the War, he found himself running across the fields a final time toward the coughing guns in front of him. It was then that the hand had reached up and grabbed him as he tried to pass. It held him tightly around his ankle, and Henry Bright did the one thing he had sworn to himself that he would never do. He looked down.

A man was looking up into his eyes. "Henry Bright," the angel said.

And then a bullet from somewhere had hit Bright in the shoulder, knocking him to the ground. Sometime later the War ended, but none of the dead got up and he couldn't get up either. He wondered if he was dead too, and he tried to prop himself up on one elbow. The stretch of pain across his arm was like crucifixion, and he had to lie back down. He began to feel as cold as the hand that had wrapped itself around his ankle.

"Angel!" he called, but if the angel heard him it didn't answer. Keeping his arms very still at his sides, he strained to sit up again. This time the hand still held his ankle fast, giving him something to pull against until he was finally in a sitting position. His teeth began to chatter. The fields around him seemed empty of life in all directions. Here and there, as if fissures had opened up in the crust of the world, puffs of smoke lifted and blew off in the breeze, but this seemed like the only movement. He called out to the angel again, but it gave no reply, and he knew somehow that it was gone.

He pulled the field dressing from the inside of his belt. There was a wax envelope filled with white powder, a bundle of lintin, two pins, and a roll of gauze. His shaking fingers dropped one of the pins on the ground, and his heart went thudding in the back of his head as he twisted to pick it up. He tried to hold the stays between his lips but his teeth wouldn't keep still, so he stuck the pins in the leather of someone's nearby boot heel. He pulled off his punctured jacket and then his bloody shirt. He poured his canteen on the wound, but he couldn't see if it was clean. His good hand looked enormous and tremendously real while it did its work, as if it belonged to a stranger. He watched it pour the waxen envelope of powder into the wound in his shoulder, and he heard the pop and sizzle of the powder as it cauterized the hole. The sound was like the small-arms fire of a faraway front line where nobody knew that the War had ended. It burned badly, the powder, and he pressed the twist of lintin into the wound and watched it turn red before his eyes. He threw it away and applied the other piece, then wrapped the gauze bandage tightly around it, managing for a few seconds to hold the end of the dressing between his chattering teeth to keep it tight until he had it pinned. Then he fell backward again and lay there looking up at a sky that was empty of shells, empty of bullets, empty of gas and planes, empty of bearded old men and beautiful girls, empty of angels.

29

The Colonel stood in the general-merchandise store puzzling over his money. On the counter lay the half box of bullets that the lady had counted out. He had spied her working alone through the window and straightened his uniform in the reflection of the glass. He'd removed his hat, run his fingers through his thin gray hair, and told his boys to wait for him outside the establishment.

"I seem to have a few mites less than the purchase price," he said to her.

"Well," the lady tried, "you could just buy fewer bullets." The old man had been standing there looking at the coins in his hand quizzically for almost a minute, as if more money might suddenly appear.

"Yes . . ." His voice trailed off, and he looked up at her as if she might have more to say on the subject.

"The rifle can't hold more than a few bullets at a time anyway, so why don't you just buy a few and then come back if you need more?"

"Contractions," the Colonel said softly.

"What?" She tapped the box of ammunition impatiently. "If it was me, that's what I'd do." A bowl of sugar cubes sat near the register.

"Was there a man in here with a baby yesterday?"

Duncan and Corwin stood watching him through the window as he questioned the lady.

"What?" The lady seemed annoyed to have the subject changed.

"Yesterday," he continued. "A father and an infant. Henry Bright is the man's name."

The lady's face softened a bit. "That poor man," she said. "His wife died, and it's only him left to care for that little boy." She shook her head and sucked in her cheeks against the bitterness of it all. "The world is a cruel place, and there's no denying it."

"A little boy," said the Colonel. "A little baby boy." His eyes drifted off the woman's face and over her shoulder at the bolts of fabric a moment before they snapped back. "It is a cruel place and there is *indeed* no denying it," he agreed.

"You're right about that," the woman said, reaffirming the fact. "Now," she said, tapping the box again, "can I help you with anything else?"

"May I?" The Colonel pointed his finger close to the sugar bowl.

She looked at the man's dirty hands and then at the clean white lumps of sugar. She took one from the bowl and placed it on the counter next to the bullets.

The Colonel took the sugar and turned toward the window, popping it in his mouth and winking for the benefit of his sons. Corwin pressed his face against the pane of glass with a beseeching look in his eyes. The Colonel turned back to the lady, his face gone somber and gray.

"I am seeking that man for something." He fixed the woman with a cold stare. He pointed at the sugar bowl again. "Might I have another lump of sugar?"

Before she could answer, there came a thud against the windowpane and sounds of a scuffle from outside. Corwin and Duncan were surrounded by six men.

The woman looked out the window and then back at the Colonel. "They're from the coal company," she said. "Making sure we don't have the wrong kinds of people staying in town too long. Are you relations?"

The Colonel glanced over his shoulder without interest at the faces of his sons. "With them? No. I have never laid eyes on them in my life," he said.

"I didn't mean with them," the woman said, frustrated. "I meant with the soldier—Henry Bright—and his boy. Are you related to the soldier and his boy?" She asked the question slowly, as if the old man was softheaded.

They both looked at the bullets there on the counter.

"Ah, yes. Henry. The man is my . . ." He chuckled to himself, then smiled thinly at the snooping old thing. "You see, the man murdered my daughter."

She threw a hand over her mouth and stared at the Colonel wide-eyed.

From outside the store rose the quick, scuffling sounds of a nascent mêlée. He listened with quiet satisfaction, but his gaze did not wander from the woman's face.

"That man?" she asked in disbelief. "The war hero?"

"Oh, yes," he said. "The man stole my daughter from me in the black of night, and less than a year later left her for dead after she delivered his child."

The woman looked vaguely off toward the door. "That nice soldier?" she asked.

"Indeed so," he said. "Will you tell me where he went?"

Her eyes watched the fighting outside vacantly.

"Please, will you tell me where Henry Bright went?" the

131

Colonel insisted. She didn't hear him, so absorbed was she with watching the fight outside her store and weighing the awful claims that the old man had made. The Colonel saw her distraction and snuck another lump of sugar into his mouth and leaned in closer across the counter. "I fear for the infant's life as well. The man is a murderer." He reached out suddenly, grabbing the woman high up on her arm. She looked away from the window and down at the hand clutching her, then up into his face. "I need to find Henry Bright," he said. "Tell me where he—"

The woman yanked back from his grasp. "Get the hell out of here!" Her face had gone purple with rage all at once, and she started around the counter toward him. She took a rake from a milk crate where a number of them were standing and knocked a stack of enameled pie plates to the floor. She swung the thing in a wide arc, missing him but sending a stuffed pheasant flying down the aisle. "I'll give you a beating for talking like that about a war hero!" She pounded the rake's handle on the floor and glared at him as two of the coal-company men entered the store. "Ralph," she said. "Edgar."

"I can see that you are a fine woman and ever the help of those in need," the Colonel said, with the last reserves of his courtly composure. Strong arms pulled him toward the shop door. "If you see that rogue again, tell him that I am going to find and kill him."

The woman followed the men to the doorway and out onto the street as they dragged the old man and his sons down toward the coal-company offices. "Make sure I don't ever see them again or I'm gonna cut them from their ears to their assholes!" She huffed in disbelief at the kinds of people there were in the world, then she dusted herself off and disappeared into the store. In another moment she came back out again and hollered up the street to the roughs. "And when you're done with them, get on back and help me bury my cash register."

The coal-company roughs tied the trio and carried them like spitted heifers out of town, dumping them finally by the train tracks running past a coal depot. They pulled out the men's pockets but found nothing of any interest. One of the roughs drew a long knife from his own belt and held it under the Colonel's nose. "You ain't coming back here again, are you?" The Colonel shifted in his ropes and turned his face away. The rough watched him a beat longer, then laughed and cut the old man's ropes, spun him around, and kicked him hard on the backside, sending him sprawling down the tracks. He threw the unloaded and useless rifle after him. "We don't want your types around here," he said.

The roughs walked, joking among themselves, back down the road the way they had come. The Colonel sat gingerly on the railroad track and watched them go, then looked at his sons where they lay, bloody and straining against the ropes that still bound them.

When he was sure the men were gone, he pulled the long brass bullet out from between his cheek and his teeth. "I thought," he said, holding it up and examining it with a jeweler's eye, "that you would both be better behaved if I left you outside of the store."

He rubbed the bullet on his sleeve and, after inspecting its gleam, he chambered the round in the rifle with a satisfying mechanical clack. Then he laid the rifle aside and looked placidly at his sons.

"Henry Bright is nearby, and I have procured the means with which to kill him." He nodded at the rifle lying by his side. "Since it is growing late and there is nothing more that can be done at present, I feel we are all in possession of a blessed space

133

of leisure time in which I might pass on to you both a few bits of instruction concerning proper manners when residing in town." This he proceeded to do, talking at length as night fell, his lecture interrupted only once when he saw the light of a train coming and he paused so that he could drag his boys one by bundled one from the tracks, lest they be cleaved in two.

30

He lay there on the battlefield with a hole in his shoulder, until
eventually he was found and moved boozily to a Red Cross tent.
A racket of haphazard marching bands moved up and down
the gruel-colored stretch of camp road at all hours. The walls
of canvas were stiff and dreary as the sky, still as paint. The nurse
came and retreated. He was woken at times by the screams of
others. When this happened, the nurse would be there, and
sometimes the doctor too. He would be given something for his
pain and would go back to sleep, wake, and eat the cool soup
that was spooned to him. There were voices outside and commotion at times. Then everything would get dark again and he
would lie there and call out to the vanished angel.

He was in the Red Cross tent for so long that it began to
seem that he might be the last one to leave the War. He got up
but was made to lie back down again. He got up again, and this
time he was put on a truck that took him to a train. The train
took him to the coast, and at the coast he was placed aboard a
steam liner. After four days of sitting in port, the steam liner
left. He never saw any of the men he had known in the trenches
again. He kept a careful watch for the Colonel's sons, but they
weren't on his boat. He found whatever solitude he could on
board. He tried closing his eyes or watching the waves as they

frothed behind the ship. He took Bert's stolen gun from his haversack and sat staring at the lettering, letting his eyes unfocus and the talk of others blur around him. None of it was any use. The angel seemed gone for good. His shoulder throbbed in the damp air. The boat landed in Virginia. He was given a ticket and got on a train that, after many stops, dropped him at the same empty station he had departed from just over a year previous.

The neglected cabin was in much need of work, but Bright began at the edges. He went into the woods and cut six trees, then spent the next two days fashioning fence posts that he placed around the small garden that his mother had made. Although it was still early in the spring and frost painted the ground each morning, he slept in his army kit in the timothy grass within sight of the cabin. He did not go in. He wasn't quite ready to resume his former life. He ate whatever he had left from his trip. He walked a half day to Fells Corner for a bar of soap, a pound of nails, and tar paper with which to patch the roof of the hen hutch. At first the old man in the hardware store didn't recognize the gaunt, uniformed young man who stood before him. When at last he did, the man came out from behind the counter and put his arms around him, and this time he gave him two full pounds of nails for free before making Bright promise to come to the auction the following week.

He returned home and hacked away the tall grass that had grown up around his mother's grave. Something—the winter snow, wild animals—had pushed inward most of the boards he had nailed over the cabin door to protect the inside from weather. He pried and yanked away whatever splinters remained nailed to the door frame, then he turned in the doorway and looked a while at the homestead he had reclaimed. When he was finally ready, he stepped inside the cabin and sat there on the bed for a very long time, as if waiting to feel something, while the hours passed and the slant of the daylight changed around him. At last he stood on the lumpy straw mattress and felt around in the shadows of the rafters for his mother's rifle. The gun was missing.

31

Come morning, his boys were a travesty to look upon. Swollen lips, black eyes, cheekbones bruised, foreheads and noses bloody and dirty. After untying them, the Colonel made his way a little farther into the forest and then up a small rise. To his left and right the trees went on to the horizon, deep blue-green and gently breathing. Directly in front of him, about a quarter mile distant, the forest of hickory and oak gave way to an enormous rectangle of lawn with several small man-made ponds strewn carelessly about. They reflected a sky that was one part daybreak and two parts smoke. The Colonel paid the impending fire no mind. His eyes were roving over the spectacular white hotel. The building was at least four hundred feet long, with drowsy, darkened windows just beginning to garner the sunlight, as if the morning was one more servant to be admitted into the room along with the coffee and the big-city papers. Tennis courts and a swimming pool were appended to the right side of the hotel, and to the extreme left, on the far side of the great lawn and set slightly back into the trees, stood a large white barn trimmed in green.

"I am going to the hotel to ask for Henry Bright," he announced to his sons when he got back to the train tracks. "I gleaned from the lady in the store that he was very close. I will see what further information I can come by there." Corwin was sitting on one of the rails, throwing small rocks at his brother's back. The struggle had gone out of Duncan, who sat staring fixedly at the sunlight glancing off one of the rails.

"From the rise there you can see a large white barn," the Colonel said, pointing. "While I am away, I want the two of you to scout it for Henry Bright's horse. If by luck you do find the animal stabled there, do not harm it." He looked hard at both of his sons to make sure that they were listening. "Allow me to emphasize. Do not harm the horse! . . . I want nothing to alert the rogue that we are nearby." The Colonel removed his uniform jacket and shook it, releasing clouds of dust into the air. "And you would both do well to otherwise keep to the woods, as you look less than presentable."

He made his way through the woods and down to the road leading through the gates to the hotel. At the foot of the hotel steps, he met a crisply dressed porter who brought him up the wide marble stairs, through an ornate revolving door, and into a large lobby with a sky-blue dome and a beautiful grand piano. Here the ragged old man was passed from the porter to an equally well-pressed bellboy, of whom the Colonel inquired where a proud grandfather might breakfast with his son and new grandson, who happened to be guests of the hotel. The bellboy smiled at him and led the way to the breakfast room. A few reverberant murmurs of conversation met the Colonel's ears from a group of departing guests as he walked by the reception desk.

". . . and so we decided to get out now while the getting out was good . . ."

". . . but I don't believe it . . ."

". . . if it is worse than '09, which they say maybe it will be . . ."

". . . never happen . . ."

The bellboy spoke over his shoulder to the Colonel. "Everything you've heard about the breakfast here is true," he said, as they passed beneath an oaken Tudor arch and into a glassed-in conservatory. The light streaming through the windows gleamed off the polished silver service and scattered brilliantly in all directions, as if the whole room were contained within a bubble in some sunlit brook. "Eggs Benedict, eggs *Florentine*"—the bellboy stretched the word out like he was describing the Grand Canyon—"eggs Benedict *with trout*? Believe me, sir, it's the best there is, and there's plenty of it." With a nod to a passing girl, he returned to the lobby and the girl led the Colonel to a setting for two near the far end of the long glass room. Nearby, a group of four young people—two men and two women—was arrayed around a table. They had stopped their talking as he approached and were now looking at him as if he was some acquaintance of theirs who had dressed in costume. The smiles of the two women were already forming as they turned back around to face the men. A chair was pulled out for the Colonel, and he brushed the seat cushion once with the napkin.

"So then . . ." he heard one of the women say, as she tried to retrieve the strand of the conversation, "so then Amelia went . . ."

"Good morning to you all," the Colonel said brightly.

"Ah, good morning," one of the men said. The other, looking directly down at his crumpet and spearing it absentmindedly with a knife, turned his head and gave the barest, most obligatory of nods before returning his attentions to the pastry.

The Colonel, after nodding respectfully at the women, turned his attentions fully upon his napkin, taking it by the corners and flipping it as if he were taunting a bull before tucking half its length into his collar.

The woman began again, "So then Amelia—"

"*I'll* tell it, Evelyn, if you don't mind, since he did propose *to me*," Amelia laughed.

"She's jealous," the truculent man said into his crumpet.

"I am jealous," Evelyn said. She turned, smiling, to the man with a fine mustache at the end of the table, who had first greeted the Colonel. "Lawrence"—she laid her hand on his arm and batted her eyelashes—"if you'd asked me to marry you, I would have said yes in a second!"

"I recall that I did ask you to marry me once, Evie," he said.

"But that was ages ago. Years. And just moments before, you'd fallen off the railing and into the garden. I chalked it up to a head injury. But if you asked me now—"

"Oh, hush," Amelia said. "He's asked me to marry him and I'm not letting him take it back, am I, Lawrence?"

"What a pleasant day for a walk," the Colonel interjected from over at his small table.

The group paused their conversation and looked at him blankly.

"Yes, it is," Amelia said after a moment, "and you look as if you've already been out walking this morning."

"About a thousand miles," the ill-natured man said with a snort.

"Now, Russell . . . manners . . . How far have you come, sir? Have you had to escape the fire too?" She twisted her hair and leaned toward him as she asked the question.

"Oh, I live just down the road, a mile back in town," the Colonel said.

"Pleasant place," Lawrence remarked. "I've been coming here since I was a boy. I've always loved it." He had on a hunting jacket with a leather patch on the shoulder for the rifle butt.

"It is an extremely pleasant place," the Colonel agreed. He motioned at the extra place setting. "I am meeting my son here for breakfast. He has just had a child." The waiting girl arrived.

141

"Coffee, black," he barked. "And steel-cut oats with canned peaches." She left. "My son is a soldier," the Colonel said, and watched their faces.

"Well, that's wonderful," Evelyn said. "Soldiers everywhere."

"Was he in France?" Amelia asked.

"Yes he was. Fighting the Boche. Am I to take by your comment that there are other veterans here besides myself and my son?"

"Were you in France too?"

"The Philippines," he said, his eyes never leaving Amelia's face. "And you said there were other veterans staying here?"

Not to be ignored, Evelyn leaned in closer. "Early this morning, a veteran in his uniform came in from the direction of the fire. He was out of his senses."

"Shouldn't have let him in," sullen Russell opined. He sat back in his chair and looked in the opposite direction from the Colonel. "He'll get the whole place sick with the mumps. That on top of the fire, on top of them letting the whole pikey hillbilly world come and stay for free until it passes? I won't be coming back here. I don't pay good money to get the mumps and eat possum stew."

"I swear, Russell, you're such a pussy willow sometimes." Amelia cocked her thumb back at her new fiancé. "You're as bad as Lawrence. After all, it was only poison ivy." She turned back to the Colonel. "Lawrence thinks I was crazy to have the man moved up out of the basement and into the hotel, but I had a nice room and he is a veteran after all, so I wanted him moved to a place where he could be absolutely comfortable. It was the very least I could do. We're leaving today anyway."

"What was the room number?" the Colonel asked. "Perhaps I will visit him before I leave. Veteran to veteran, you know."

"Oh, dear, I don't have any idea. There are no room numbers on the top floor, are there, Lawrence?"

"I haven't got the foggiest," Lawrence said, grown bored.

The group drifted back into their own conversation, and the room filled with the boisterous laughter of men about to go out for a last round of golf or shooting before they all got in their cars to drive away and escape the fire. As he ate and drank his coffee, the Colonel listened for further word of Henry Bright, but he heard nothing.

Before the bill could be brought, he stood and bowed to his neighbors. "Have a blessed day," he said sweetly. Holding his paper-white palms out toward Amelia, he took her hands in his and bent low across the breakfast table to kiss them. "May your impending union be as fruitful as my son's has been." He nodded once more at Lawrence, who returned the nod sternly. Then, with great and gathered dignity, he walked across the breakfast-room floor and out into the smoke-filled morning to go find his sons and fetch his rifle.

32

For the next few days after he arrived home, Bright worked
steadily at making more repairs. He cleared the garden patch,
beating back the intruding tendrils of the wilderness and in
the process exhuming nearly a bushel of homuncular carrots.
He climbed up on the roof and repapered with the tar paper he
had bought at the hardware store, then he chipped some new
shingles from the pitchy remnants of the fence posts he had set
around the garden. He removed the contents of the cabin and
placed them in the yard: the enameled washbasin, the trunk for
his mother's clothes, the mahogany credenza, the moldering
Bible, and the bed. He swept out the cabin's lantern-blacked interior, then filled the bucket with water and used a rag to work
the deep dirt out of the floorboards. When he was done, he
stripped off his clothes and washed in the stream. Then he
shaved, climbed into his uniform, and set off to Fells Corner for
the auction. Though he'd dumped the bullets on the ground
back in the War, he held Bert's beautiful stolen gun in his hand,
visible to anyone who might be watching him from the woods
as he passed the house where the Colonel and his sons lived.
Once he was down the road a ways, he tucked the gun back
into his haversack.

He was unprepared for the stir he would make at the auction. Since he'd returned from France, he'd spoken to no one but the conductor on the train and the man at the hardware store. After such long silence, the little town at auction time was a nightmare of back slaps, hand-wringing, tears, and canned fruit. A fat little man with a straw hat and a blueberry stain on his shirt turned out to be the mayor. He stood on a crate, clasped Bright's hand above his head, and made a speech. Everywhere Bright went, small boys followed him around, patrolling left and right and using the same kind of talk that Bert had before he was shot in the head. Old men saluted him and young men watched him from the corners of their eyes.

The auctioneer referred to him as "our very own" each time Bright raised his hand to place a bid. He bought the hens first, then the two white goats. He went outside and ate some fried chicken that was given to him and drank a mug of beer and a cup of buttermilk. He ate a piece of pie that had been brought to him by a detachment of flat-chested girls. When he was done, he got up from the picnic table and went back into the sweat and tobacco of the auction hall to examine the horses.

33

The Colonel arrived back at the train tracks near the coal depot where they had spent the night to find his sons squatted around a desultory fire, tearing at an unplucked chicken carcass. He eyed the two boys closely. Corwin glanced up dully, then returned to his meal. Duncan received his father's gaze in his bottomless black eyes. After a moment the old man looked away, then turned to Corwin. "Report," he commanded.

"We found a chicken," Corwin said, his mouth around a bone.

"I can see that. Where?"

Corwin ducked his head in the direction. "The barn. They got a bunch of them there if you want to go get one."

The Colonel sniffed at this. "I am not asking because I wish to pilfer a chicken. I have already taken my breakfast. I had steel-cut oats with peaches and cream."

Corwin's fingers were sticky with down and chicken blood. "Peaches?" he asked. He wiped his index finger and thumb on his pant leg, but none of the grime came away.

"Peaches in syrup, yes."

"I've never had a peach."

"It would be wasted on you."

"No, it wouldn't!"

"In any case, you will never have the chance. The two of you could never behave yourselves in such fine company as take their breakfast yonder. Now report," he said again.

Duncan watched his brother throw a chicken bone off into the weeds by the train track. "A man was there. We watched him through the trees. He had Henry Bright's horse and he was brushing it and then he took it into the barn."

"How do you know for sure that it was the rogue's horse?"

"Because he also had his goat there on a rope. I know it was his goat. Corwin and I seen it once."

Corwin nodded at the memory, breathing through his mouth.

The Colonel sighed in contentment over the peaches in his belly, no longer listening to the story. He looked for a while through the trees in the direction of the hotel. Then, as if a great notion had come into his mind, he turned back to his sons. "Would you like some peaches after all, Corwin?"

"You know I do!" Corwin said.

"Of course you do." The Colonel smiled. He stooped to pick up the rifle and began walking down the tracks in the direction of the coal depot. Corwin jumped up and followed his father, leaving what was left of the wretched chicken body to blow forlornly in the morning breeze between the rails.

Duncan looked at the fire gathering strength behind the trees. Then he stood and followed, rubbing the small of his back where it was sore from his relations and other kinds of people kicking him and throwing rocks at him.

34

When Bright woke again, the curtains were drawn wide and muted morning light suffused the room. A kind of woman entirely unknown to him sat slung across a burgundy divan.

"*You* have been talking in your sleep," she said. Her dark-yellow hair hung heavily about her face as if freshly forged. She looked at him amusedly.

"What did I say?" he asked, his eyes roving about the room for the cook, Brigid. The carpets were thick and beige colored. At either end, body-length mirrors in japanned frames reflected back and forth upon each other.

"Oh, all of your secrets are safe with me, H. Bright," the woman said. She vaulted to her feet and came to stand at the head of his bed, shooting a hand toward him. "Amelia," she said. "My last name is Choate, A. Choate. And you are H. Bright."

The bed squeaked as he took her hand.

"There," she said. "Formalities laid to rest. Now, just lie back and let me talk." She leaned over him, peering closely at the rash on his face. "Cripes. They say the water here is healthful, so maybe you've come to the right place. I see you've noticed my ring. Ha. It's black pearl. Not at all so rare as Lawrence would have me believe, but I don't tell him this, of course, because all that kind of talk is so dull. Anyway, if he really is serious about marrying me this time, which I can't help but think he is, then he'll have to cough up for something much flashier soon enough. I'm talking diamonds, H. Not that I care. I don't wear much jewelry. I'm wearing this at the moment only because he's just given it to me. Now he's out shooting birds with his 'pals.'"

She ran a hand through her hair. "I was invited to join them too, of course. I'm actually quite a good shot, but that would mean me spending more time with his 'pals,' and so I told him that I was going to head back upstairs to make the acquaintance of my war hero, H. Bright." She regarded him with a cocked eyebrow. "Dear H., can't you see that I'm trying to get it through your head that you haven't introduced yourself to me yet? Your last name was easy, it's written on your uniform. I was in school with an Alexandra Bright. We called her Flexy."

"My name is Henry," he said. "Where is my boy at?"

Amelia looked hard at him, as if he'd said something unexpectedly cruel. Then her face changed and she let out a small sigh. "Ah. Henry. I see. Then I hope that you won't mind me calling you H. It's not your fault, it's just that a certain other Henry was the author of a disastrous chapter in my life, and the memory is a bit . . . fresh . . . yet." She gave a short laugh and looked down at the bedspread.

"Isn't it funny, don't you think, how at times one can't escape a name? There was a year when it seemed that every new man that I met was named Albert, or Bertie, or Bert. Large-footed, husky dolts, to a one, but I couldn't escape that name. There's a riddle in it somehow, or perhaps it was my subconscious telling me that I needed to be with a strong, simple-minded, Teutonic sort."

149

"I knew a Bert," he said. "In the War. Where's my boy?" he asked her again.

"Oh, H.! I'm sorry. I'm going on and on, and all the while the forest fire really is coming close. Well, I'm getting out," she said. "Still, there's a part of me wishes I could stay here and help fight it. Your boy. Yes. Your boy is being cared for by one of the cooks. He'll break hearts for sure." She tapped her ring finger on the wooden headboard and winked down at him. "Like you, H., like you."

"He's all right?"

"Of course he's all right! He's in the pink! The doctor has been in checking on you both. He's from Baltimore. They say he's the best there is in nem-... pom-... I don't know, something-something-ology. Anyway, he said it was poison ivy."

There came a knock at the door. Amelia peered through the peephole and then swung the door open for Brigid to enter. "Ah! The soup! Just put it over there to cool, and you can come in and feed Mr. Bright when I'm through with him."

Brigid set the steaming bowl on a side table and stopped to readjust the covers at the bottom of the bed. Again Bright noticed the rough redness of her hands.

"Thank you, thank you," Amelia said, holding the door open for the departing girl.

"Is my boy all right?" he asked loudly. The exhaustion and anxiety welled up plainly in his voice.

Brigid turned back and nodded. "He's fine." There was a long pause as she stole a glance at Amelia and then back at Bright. "Try to rest now." She turned again to leave. The smoke outside waved across the room at itself in the facing reflections of the japanned mirrors.

"My horse and my goat?" he asked after her.

"They're both fine as well. We've kept them at the barn, but if the fire gets closer, Dennis will make sure they're moved. Now, don't worry. I'll bring your boy up to say hello in just a little bit."

She let the door hang open a crack when she left the room. Amelia crossed the floor and pushed it firmly closed.

"I like her," she said, rapping her ring on the doorknob. "Now, tell me, H." She walked across the room and stood at the foot of his bed. "What was it like?"

"What was what like?"

"Oh, don't be like that. What was *it* like? The War? Come, now, no one gets to be my war hero unless they tell me what it was that they did in the War."

"The War?"

"All right," she laughed. "I'm too proud to wheedle it out of you, H. My things are being packed while Lawrence is out shooting at quails or ducks or geese or whatever, but I'll be back to say goodbye when he's ready to go. When I get back, I expect at least one ripping good yarn. And see if you can work in that Patton fellow," she added. "I think he is absolutely a man."

She put her hand on the knob, but she stood still and did not turn it. "My first husband went, you know," she said, not looking at him. "He wasn't actually my husband, not yet, but we were going to be married. He died. I was there with his family when the man came. He said that Henry—yes, that was his name, H., *Henry*: horrible, isn't it?—had perished a hero. 'Perished?' I asked the man. 'Yes,' he said. 'Perished.' I asked him how and the man said that that was all he could tell me. He told me that he was loved by his men and that he had perished a hero. I said, 'Well, of course he was loved by his men. Of course he perished a hero. How else could he have perished?'"

She toed the plush silver carpet, her face impassive. "Lawrence didn't go," she said. "He has a trick shoulder, but keeping him out of the War is the only trick I've seen it do." She opened the door. "I'm sorry," she said. "I'm spilling my guts all over you."

Henry Bright had had guts spilled on him before, and he said nothing.

35

The fire pushed them all before it, eastward, through the hardwoods to the coal-company town. They carried everything they could with them: heirlooms and axes, tin washbasins and butter churns. Whatever couldn't be carried by hand was lashed to livestock. There were a few spluttering automobiles, but mostly it was mules and doze-eyed oxen dragging wagons, horses carrying the infirm.

Upon arriving in the coal-company town, the refugees found a prosperous place coming apart at its seams. The pale, frightened faces of children peeked out from the shadows behind screen doors. Men soaked their lawns and roofs with water in the hopes that the fire might not be able to catch hold. Women piled precious belongings in the street, torn between what could be taken and what would be left to burn.

Rumors that had been gusting about on the dry wind could now be confirmed by the new arrivals. Fells Corner was gone. Its inhabitants had tried briefly to save it, but what had initially been a small blaze had quickly grown monstrous on great drafts of air and the summer heat. There had followed a chaotic period of making ready to leave, and by the time that they finally abandoned town, the fire was crowning and there was scarcely time for a last look back.

After that it had come down to simply trying to stay ahead of the blaze. They traveled along the train tracks through cold-mouthed railroad tunnels and across the perilous high trestles that seemed to creak and sway with vertigo beneath them. Even as they crossed the final one, the stragglers had seen the flames licking at its stanchions, the rising odor of boiling pitch and creosote like burnt black licorice in their noses.

The coal-company town, racked by a panic of its own, could offer no help or shelter to this smoke-stained group except to point them down the road toward the wide open lawn of the hotel. So they came through the hotel gates in ragged, stumbling clumps of humans, animals, and housewares, casting themselves upon the safety of the great green field, milling about like people awaking from a single shared nightmare.

In the midst of this strange scene, no one took much notice of the three bedraggled men, hands and faces deeply stained with soot, who shambled out of the woods and onto the lawn toward the gushing fountain at the front of the hotel. Once there, the three did not get in line to wash their faces in the water but instead hung closely together. When at last the eldest, a graying man with a rifle slung over his back, did peel away from the other two, it was in order to address a young woman who wore the uniform of a cook. The young woman carried an infant hugged securely against her inside a white sling. She nodded at what the soot-covered man said before motioning him along toward a sandy-haired man who was directing another group of refugees into the hotel. A smile played itself across the old man's blackened face as he bowed low to her, but the girl had already turned away and was now talking with someone else, her hand brushing absently at the birthmark on her temple.

36

When the auctioneer held up Bert's stolen German pistol, the auction hall gasped. The bidding was higher than expected, but in the end a man from Lewisburg, a doctor, purchased it. With the money he made, Bright bought a black horse, about twenty years old with decent teeth, freshly shod hooves, and a back only slightly bowed considering the size of the farmer putting it up for sale. He slept soundly that night in the barn of the hardware-store man, with a full belly, four chickens, two goats, and the horse.

It was raining the next morning as he and his band of animals began the trip homeward. He tied the chicken crates to the horse's back and strung the goats in a caravan behind the horse. The goats were meddlesome creatures and the horse, bored, stupid, or both, didn't resist them when they chose to go their own way. As a result, the big animal's plodding hindquarters would gradually drift sideways toward whatever leafy green the little white goats had a taste for. A passerby would have wondered at the group: a skinny, uniformed young man leading a horse that seemed to be learning the difficult art of walking sideways in a steady downpour. Eventually Bright untied them from the horse and briefly tried pulling them down the road separately, holding their tethers in his free hand. In the end, though, he let them off their leads entirely and left them to follow him as he and his horse continued trudging down the muddy road.

They stayed close at first, but as he passed the overgrown wagon-wheel tracks that were the turnoff to the Colonel's house, the she-goat hung back to munch and nose the tall grass and nettles of the drive. After a hundred yards she had made no signs of rejoining the group. He pulled the horse to a halt and waited for her to emerge. When she did not, he retethered the billy goat and led his remaining animals down the road to stand once more at the turnoff. It was all very quiet, save for the quizzical clucking of the chickens and the raindrops against the leaves. He thought of how his mother always had her rifle with her when they passed the drive. He remembered how they used to meet Rachel here each morning before school and how Duncan had stood in this very spot on that terrible day of the rabbits and chickens. He wished briefly to have Bert's gun back. When he could no longer help it, he let his mind linger on the French farmhouse and the things he had seen inside it.

He began walking up the drive, pulling the animals behind him and clicking his tongue softly for the she-goat as he peered through the dripping foliage. There was nothing around the first bend but the rain and yet another bend. Around this second corner, the road softened into a wet marsh of cattails and devil's walking stick and the house hove into view. The lawn was mangy gray, the brittle needles of grass grown high and spiky. A rust-colored stream ran along the far southern edge of the plot, and what few trees remained between the stream and the house seemed like overgrown twins of the grass. Their branches were hacked crudely away up to forty feet, past which point they spindled outward like finger bones. The wrought-iron balcony listed dangerously out of plumb, the ivy vines hanging thickly from it pulling it to the ground like some waxen green lion. It was here, beneath the balcony, that he saw Rachel. She was standing so motionless in the shadows that at first glance he had taken her for an off-white warping in the moldering clapboard. She was watching something that was happening in the mud-packed wasteland out of view on the other side of the house. He moved farther out onto the drive, hoping for a better angle in which to see the girl, and caught his breath on what he saw instead.

Corwin had scooped up the she-goat in his cumbersome arms, and reedy, underfed Duncan stood close by, holding a clump of yellow grass under her nose. Her tail flicked and looped in the air like a distress flag.

Rachel had noticed him now. He stared back at her, forgetting his goat and the Colonel's sons. She was far too skinny. Around her waist the white dress hung loosely, and her shoulders were scarcely wide enough to keep it from slipping off. Her collarbones were almost avian, painful to behold. When at last the moment passed and he looked over at the two men holding his goat, he thought of them standing above him in the darkness as he lay beneath Bert's body in the ditch during the War.

Together, the group formed a haphazard nativity scene in the rain-soaked yard.

"That's my goat," he said. "I bought her in Fells Corner. At the auction there. There's more like her if you want your own."

The goat began to squirm and kick its stony hooves against Corwin's chest. "I want my goat back," he said again. "Please."

Rachel looked once behind her into the recesses of the house and then at her brothers. "Give it back," she said quietly. "Give it back. That's Henry's goat so don't you be fiddling with it anymore."

Corwin gave his sister a cloying smile and set the goat on the ground with exaggerated care, as if it were a china dish. He backed away from the animal, extending his arms in invitation

157

to Bright. Bright came forward to pick it up, but his eyes never left the two men. "Thank you," he said. He held the goat tightly so that they would not see his hands shaking.

"Henry?" Rachel tilted her head with the question. "Henry, where have you been?"

He didn't know what to say. Her face was so beautiful to him that she made her surroundings look all the more deplorable. "I went to the War," he stammered. "I was in the War." He stole a glance at Corwin and Duncan as he said it.

"Did you get married there, Henry?" she asked. "I bet you did. I bet you got married there."

He swallowed drily. After a pause he said, "No. No, I just stayed there and that's all I did." He nodded to Corwin and Duncan. Neither returned the nod. He nodded at Rachel, then turned and pulled his animals out of the yard, down the drive, and back through the rain to the main road and his cabin.

The angel gave him no peace after that.

37

The Colonel and his sons, another old man, two elderly women, four or five young couples, and an indiscriminate number of children and dogs followed the hotel man named Dennis down a long basement hallway and into a large concrete room. A metallic click came as Dennis flipped a switch, and the few electric bulbs cast their light dimly on rows of mattresses lined up on the stone floor. One of the old women had breathed in too much smoke from the fire, and every time she began to cough, one of the dogs would bark. As soon as Dennis left, Duncan went immediately to a bed in the far corner of the room and lay down, putting the thin pillow over his head to keep out the noise. The Colonel sank down against the wall and pulled his hat over his eyes to think.

He had expected that his army uniform would have more of an effect on the cook he had talked to by the fountain and that, in return for the service he had given to his country, she would have sent him upstairs to rest in one of the resplendent rooms on the top floor, as Henry Bright had been. The young woman had a birthmark on her temple and had been carrying a newborn. He had congratulated her on her beautiful child and had not missed the brief look of confusion there in her eyes. Now he sat on the floor in the basement with the loaded rifle across his knees, pondering how best to find Henry Bright now that he had located both the rogue's horse and his child.

The man who owned the hardware store in Fells Corner stood across the room staring at the Colonel, then walked over and nudged the sitting figure with his boot. The Colonel shifted his hat toward the back of his head and lifted his eyes to return the store owner's glare.

"You don't remember me," the Fells Corner man said. There was spite in his voice.

"Of course I do," the Colonel replied with equal spite.

"We ain't gonna have any trouble with you or them boys. Not today." His voice was flat. "Git."

The Colonel sighed. "Sir, I am a colonel and expect to be addressed with the courtesy due me." He pulled the hat back over his eyes. "As befits my rank," he added.

"If you're a colonel, I'm George Washington," the hardware man said to the brim of the Colonel's hat. An old woman cackled loudly, then began to cough. A dog started barking. "We ain't gonna have your boys in the same room as the children or the women. We all got enough trouble already. Git." He toed the Colonel once again, harder this time.

By the time Dennis returned to the basement room, leading more refugees, three men had ahold of Corwin and another held Duncan's arms behind his back. The hardware-store man was leaning forward on the balls of his feet, jabbing a peglike finger into the Colonel's chest while the Colonel looked derisively at his tormentor over coal-smeared cheekbones.

Dennis stopped in the doorway. "What's this?" The people he was leading went on tiptoe behind him trying to catch a glimpse.

At the sound of Dennis's voice, the Colonel pivoted slowly to face him, showing his back to the Fells Corner hardware man. "There are peasants in my lodgings," he said. "Fleas and the croup are rampant. Children and dogs have overrun the place."

"These ones ain't staying here," one of the men holding Corwin said to Dennis. "Not inside with the children or the women."

"Or the dogs!" someone else yelled.

The hardware-store man went on: "They live over near where we come from. Believe me, there's nothing about these ones that ain't wrong."

"They might even've started the fire," said the big man holding Duncan. He had a thick pink scar running through his right eyebrow. "They ain't staying here." He twisted Duncan's arms hard, as if to emphasize the point. Duncan's body seemed to slacken against the pain, then all of a sudden he jerked back, butting his captor up under his chin with the crown of his head. The man winced in pain and let go of Duncan's arms, grabbing a hank of his black hair and spinning him around. He rammed the heel of his hand into Duncan's nose, releasing a spurt of blood and sending him to his hands and knees on the concrete floor. The man hauled his boot back and kicked him in the stomach. Duncan curled into a gulping, gasping ball at his feet. The man was about to kick once more when Dennis stepped forward and put a hand on his shoulder.

"You do that again, you can all find somewhere else to stay."

The man appeared to consider the option, then lowered his foot.

The Colonel looked at his son there on the cold floor and began to smile faintly to himself. He came to stand by Dennis. "I need my own room," he said. "On the top floor. With the other veteran."

Dennis knelt to help Duncan to his feet. Duncan stood, running a dirty sleeve across his nose. He looked at the red-stained arm as if it did not belong to him.

"I have come to a decision!" The Colonel's voice suddenly escalated to shrill oratory, as if he was reciting epic poetry. "Of my own volition and for no other reason, I will send my boys to stay in the barn. They will be of no trouble to you good people." He pivoted in a martial style to regard Dennis and the hardware man at once. "Is this agreeable to all parties?"

"That's not the safest place for them to be," Dennis said. "The fire will get there pretty quick. I was heading out there soon to fetch the animals closer in."

"My boys are no cowards and are no strangers to livestock. I hope they can be of some assistance in that regard."

Dennis looked at the hardware man, who shrugged back at him. "Not my animals out there," he said. He nodded at the men holding Corwin and they let go of his giant, sloped shoulders.

"Both of you go to the barn," the Colonel commanded loudly. "Stay there until you can either be of use or until the fire burns you out." After a beat he added, "Mind the chickens, but keep special watch over the horse and goat belonging to the veteran." He ran his tongue over his teeth in thought, then added, "I expect them kept safe, do you hear me?"

Corwin made for the basement door. The Colonel fixed Duncan with a dismissive look. The boy looked back at his father, his upper lip still wet with blood, then over at Dennis, and finally at the basement doorway through which Corwin had just passed. Then he walked through the group of Fells Corner men as if he had turned to shadow.

The Colonel returned his attentions to Dennis. "As for myself," he said, "I shall take a room on the top floor, as—"

"Go and talk to Brigid down the hall in the kitchen," Dennis interrupted. "Maybe she can help you like she helped the other fella."

"*Git,*" the hardware man said, and spat on the Colonel's boot.

38

It was sometime in the late afternoon when he felt strong enough to rise. His uniform was ready for him on a chair, the freshly pressed trousers and jacket hanging over its back, his underwear, shirt, and socks folded in a neat pile on the seat cushion. Atop the pile lay the ivory comb. Someone had stitched closed the bullet hole in the jacket's shoulder with black thread. He stepped into the trousers and boots, then paused before buttoning his shirt to smell a sleeve. The soap had left a scent behind that he remembered. Lemons.

He pulled the shirt on gingerly over the welts on his chest and then picked up his mother's comb. Somehow the fragile thing had survived the nightmare of the last few days. The ivory woman, whose kneeling, hand-clasped body formed its handle, looked just as composed now as she had when he had run the comb through Rachel's hair for the last time. He held it up and looked for cracks in the delicate tines, but the light was not strong enough and so he took it to the window.

A cursory knock sounded at the door and Amelia strolled into the room. "H.! How wonderful that you're up and about! And just in time too, just in the nick of time. You're watching the fire. How dreadful! Let's watch it together a moment, just you and me." The windows gazed out upon the lawn and the white barn in the distance. The sky was too dark for afternoon, and where the sun should have hung there was now only an undulating black curtain of heat which pulsed through the windowpanes upon his face like the throb of an open furnace. "I'm leaving," she said. "They say the time to leave is now or never, so now that Lawrence is done shooting at birds, he's gone to fetch the car."

He raised a knuckle to his teeth. "Where are you going?"

"Oh, back to Washington. Back to Washington and then to get married. All that. There's no more putting it off." A new crowd of people was coming through the gates on the far edge of the lawn. Carts and horses were laden with family possessions. "He wants to be a diplomat, does Lawrence," she mused. "He will be too, I'm sure. Which means moving someplace dreadful. Indochina, Indonesia, Indiana, who knows." She shook her head. "I mean, really—shooting at birds."

The big pumper engine that they had brought down from the coal mine to fight the fire had gotten stuck in the grass. Henry watched them pushing it forward and back. It belched smoke that was even blacker than the fire as the wheels rocked ineffectually in the soft earth.

It flashed into his mind suddenly that perhaps he had never left the War at all. Maybe, in fact, the War had never ended. It was impossible, standing here, to tell. The flames, the men with shovels, the people who had lost their homes and now stood clutched together, their faces chapped from the heat and windblown . . . He grabbed a hank of the curtain for support and hung on to it. His body still lay on the field where it had fallen. He was floating above it, looking down.

Amelia's voice was lost amid the particulate sift of dust raining down on his helmet, the punch of mortars, the gasp of his own breath as he labored to pull air through his gas mask.

He thought of the Colonel, that looming, constant presence,

and of Duncan and Corwin, whose atrocities had followed him ever since that awful night when they had come out of the French farmhouse and stood above him, jamming dirty fingers in his mouth.

The War, the fire, the Colonel, and the angel: It felt as if some gigantic stone had somehow dislodged itself and begun rolling toward him down the long, slow curve of the world. Soon it would catch up to him, run him and his little boy down, crush them flat, plow them under. He opened his eyes.

Down in the drive, beautiful, shining automobiles were being frantically packed. "I told Lawrence I was going to say goodbye to you and then go find a flask of something for the road. I've been gone so long he probably thinks you've made off with me."

"You've got to take my boy with you," he said suddenly.

"What?"

"When you go, you have to take my son with you," he said again. "Take him away from all of this." He nodded out the window. "He don't need me. He needs a mother."

She looked at him in frank bewilderment.

"Like Bithiah," he added. "She was the Pharaoh's daughter."

"You're talking nonsense, H. I can't do that. I think you need to lie down."

He reached into his pocket and pulled out the comb. "Take him with you. When he's older, give this to him. Tell him it was his grandmother's."

"You're cracked, H."

"Please," he said. "Just take my boy with you. Be a mother to my boy. I can't . . . I can't care for him."

"Listen, H." She pushed the comb away and, reaching up, took his face in her palms. "Listen to me now. Everything is going to be *all right*. It will be *all right*. I don't know what happened to you out there. I won't ever know, but I do know you made it to

166

safety. The fire can't reach you here. You're beyond it now and you're safe, do you hear me? Do you hear me, H.?" She glanced out the window and then back at him. "And *please* don't worry about your boy. He's in good hands and, anyway, even if the fire does come, Lawrence says there will be plenty of caravans to take everyone away."

"You don't understand."

"No, I certainly don't." She smiled sadly and patted his cheek, then took a deep breath. "Anyway, on to business. I've arranged it with the manager, and you can stay here as long as you wish. I'd recommend you do too. You look terrible, H. Get some rest and see how you feel in a few days. Order room service. I have to leave," she said. "Goodbye, Henry."

39

The silver and coffee pantries were deserted, but the Colonel found the girl he was looking for in the food pantry. The wood and metal room was cool and dark, about half the size of a boxcar, and lined, floor to ceiling, with shelves and shelves of peach, plum, and cherry preserves; flour and cornmeal; pickles and relish; canned goods of every kind; cheese wheels and sugar cubes; pats, sticks, and baker's blocks of butter; pitchers of cream; bags of salt. To his left the wall was taken up with utensils—bread knives, wooden pails, a sugar dredge, can openers, knife polishers, colanders, strainers, a hot-water urn, and various contraptions whose uses were a mystery to the old man. She had her back turned to him as he came to lean against the tin door frame. His eyes wandered over the food before resting on the damp wisps of hair that whorled at the back of the girl's neck. After a time he rapped against the floor with the rifle butt. She started and turned. The infant slept in a sling against her chest.

"The man suggested that I speak with you about being moved to quarters on the top floor of the hotel." She seemed in a spell as she looked at the gun in his hands. He rapped the rifle butt sharply on the ground once more, and she came back to herself. "Are you unwell, child?"

Her face had taken on the soft glisten of candle wax in the light of the nearest ceiling bulb. "I'm sorry," she said. "I'm just worn out. Excuse me." She walked toward the doorway, but he did not step aside. She swallowed twice convulsively, fear flooding her chest. "Excuse me, please."

"It would appear as if my boys and I brought the fire to your very door," he said. "You have been so kind to us and all the other unfortunates—my boys and me, the young veteran and his infant son on the top floor. Such kindness." He stepped across the threshold into the pantry with her, pulling the door gently closed behind him until it latched with a galvanic click.

She looked at the wall of knives, knowing that he had followed her gaze even as she did so. "I . . ." she said, blinking. The blades hung within reach, swaying and winking slightly at her. She could have lunged for one, reached out and grabbed one—she knew each of them, their feel, their balance and weight—but instead she felt her arms wrap themselves protectively around Henry Bright's son.

The Colonel flicked the light switch off. In the sudden darkness she felt him step between her and the knives on the wall. For a long moment the two listened to each other breathing in the blackness.

"A story," he began. "Once there was a good-hearted soldier, a hero, who, having served his country, retired from the battlefield in order to till the land and raise up a family. Having married the beautiful sister of a dearly departed comrade, he settled down with her to raise a family. The other sister, jealous of her fairer sibling, married a vagrant, sometime coal miner and gave birth to a rogue."

She heard the singing sound of the blades as the Colonel leaned back against the wall of knives. "As for the good-hearted man, he and his beloved wife had three beautiful children: two handsome sons and a pretty daughter, who was the man's dar-

169

ling. When his wife died, this good-hearted man, now a widower, found the great solace of his life in watching his children grow, especially the girl, who was beyond compare in beauty and virtue. As the years passed she became ever more radiant, grew up indeed into a beautiful, chaste young woman." He paused and listened for her. "Are you still there, child?"

Her voice came smally. "Yes."

"Good," he said. "Good. Now then, do you remember the rogue born of the ugly sister? Well, the rogue grew up too, but not into a proud young man, no. He grew up into something awful. Into a monster. And then, one night a year ago, without warning, he rode his horse to the old man's house, woke the old man and his children from their sleep, and, with some combination of enchantment and violence, abducted the old man's beautiful daughter and took her away to live with him in the same maggot-strewn ditch where he himself had been raised.

"In the blink of an eye, his dreams of a happy old age vanished and he saw himself for what he really was: just a foolish old man."

He coughed. "I am sorry, Miss Brigid. The smoke of the fire," he said. He flipped on the light switch. The barrel of the rifle was only a few inches from her forehead. She opened her mouth, but no sound came out. He coughed once more. "Would it be too much, do you think, to ask you for a drop of that cognac I saw there? I have not had cognac in a very, very, very long time." He motioned with his head to a dusty bottle sitting low on a shelf. "If it is not too much to ask." He looked at her expectantly. She stood paralyzed, unsure of what he meant for her to do. He cocked his head once more toward the bottle and she knelt slowly to retrieve it. He followed her with the rifle barrel as she stood back up. "The stopper," he said. "Please."

She pulled the stopper from the bottle. At the sound of the release, the baby woke in her arms and began to keen.

He shifted the rifle unsteadily to one hand and held the other out to her. "Hand it to me," he said. He took the bottle and lifted it halfway to his lips. Here he paused, however, and considered her. "Step forward," he said.

Again it was as if she couldn't move.

"Step. Forward." The barrel of the gun was only inches from her. "If you do not step forward, I will kill my grandson."

She came forward an inch.

"Good, good," the Colonel said approvingly. He beckoned. "Forward still. Forward, forward, turn your head just a bit, my dear . . . and . . . good."

When she stopped, the barrel was pressed flatly against the birthmark at her temple. The baby cried. It hurt her to hear it, but she did not move.

"Now," he said. "I have come a long way and I am going to take a drink of this rare old cognac."

He took three long swallows and then held the bottle out to her. "Take a sip yourself, child. You look as though you need it."

The rifle stock appeared to sigh against her skull as she obeyed.

She took the bottle, put it to her lips and sipped.

Abruptly, he switched the lights off again, and the room was submerged once more in blackness.

"The old man made up his mind that he would kill the rogue and bring his daughter back home where she belonged. It was right that the rogue should die. It was strange, though—each time the old man and his sons crossed the ridge with the intention of killing him, something always thwarted them. Once the old man was about to shoot, when the rogue's horse came and stood in the path of the shot. Another time, the old man's sons got into a nest of bees and were stung frightfully. He actually managed to pull the trigger once, only to find that the rifle contained no bullets. The old man would not be deterred, however. He would have his revenge. Then, one day, as he watched his daughter from the woods, he saw that she was with child and a thought came to him."

There was silence. The rifle barrel lifted from her temple in the dark, and the man's voice drew much closer. "He thought to himself, 'As the rogue has stolen my child, so, too, will I steal a child from the rogue.' He decided that he would not kill the rogue until the baby was born. Then, when the child was delivered, he would swoop down and exact his vengeance. The old man made a vow to himself that he would stand victoriously above the rogue, holding the rogue's child in his arms.

"The bottle, please," he sighed. She felt his hand grope down her arm to the bottle. He took it, gulping loudly in the dark.

The pantry could not have been darker had she closed her eyes. She tried to listen through the thick, velvet blackness, through the pantry's stone walls and metal door, for the sounds of someone who might come to her aid. She knew it was useless; the kitchen staff, the coffee and cocoa girl, the dishwashers, the stewards and waiters, had been dismissed to see to their own families, and anyone else who was still here had been set to work out on the lawn. Her thoughts flashed to Dennis, but he was probably gone to the barn to fetch the animals. "Please," she began to whisper. "Please. Please."

"Shush," the Colonel said, his grammar slipping as he drank. "Shush. A little more and then we'll both go, I reckon." He giggled. "Yeah, we'll both get going, I reckon. Anyway, the girl grew and grew with the child in her belly, and then one day she felt the pains."

His breath was at her ear now, the liquor misting on her

cheek. She backed up and he moved with her, crowding against her until her shoulder blades were pressed against the shelving on the far side of the room.

"The old man knew it," he said. "When his daughter started feeling the birth pains, he knew. He waited, and the birds of the forest stopped singing and waited with him." His throat clicked drily in her ear. "But he was never to be reunited with his daughter. She died in the early morning, delivering a son. Henry Bright set fire to the cabin and escaped to the east on his horse, carrying the baby boy that is now in your arms."

The bottle shattered against the wall where he threw it among the jars of preserves. "Where is he?" She bolted in the darkness for the door, but the Colonel caught her by her hair, looping it around his fist like reins, forcing her to her knees on the tiled floor.

"I don't know!"

He twisted her hair tightly, as if winding a spring.

"Well," he said. He was breathing hard through his mouth when he put his lips to her ear again. "I found his horse." His grip on her hair loosened for an instant. "And I found his boy." He brought the rifle butt down hard against the back of her head. She slumped, but he held her kneeling body upright by the hair so that she would not fall forward on top of the baby. "I suppose I will find him, too, soon enough." He eased her down against a shelf before switching on the light. He knelt by her, peering closely for the first time at his daughter's child. Its eyes were tightly closed, but it was giving full throat to its displeasure. He lifted the cooking girl's arm so that he could pull the infant in its sling from around her neck and hang it round his own. Then he stood and opened the pantry door to the brightness of the kitchen.

The ridiculous young woman he had met at breakfast was

sloshing whiskey into a silver flask over the sink. "Well, hello," she said brightly. "We meet again. I was just finding Lawrence and me a drink to take with us for the road."

Without a word, the Colonel carried the screaming infant past her. He threw open the door of the servants' entrance, and the child's howls folded into the howling of the wind as it whipped around the hotel eaves and into the room, setting the hanging pots and pans to rattling and banging against one an-other. He stood looking out at the lawn, with its great crowd of people and cars, dogs and horses. In the space above his head, the doorway framed the fire crowning in the treetops. Flames lashed at the trees, tearing branches away, hurling them sky-ward in great updrafts. The barn stood nestled in their midst, glowing like an in got of white-hot metal. He looked steadily at the far-off building, watching it closely even as a cinder the size of a man's leg fell out of the sky at his feet in the doorway. All at once he seemed to come to a decision, and clamping an arm around the crying child on his chest, he pulled the rifle tightly against his back and started out across the lawn.

Pots were falling off the wall now, and somehow a sack of flour had been knocked to the floor and exploded open. The fine white powder was swept up into the currents of air and swirled angrily around the room like a trapped ghost. Amelia dropped the whiskey bottle and the flask in the sink and grabbed the nearest pot, throwing it under the tap and filling it with water. She ran to the burning branch that had landed in the doorway and doused it. The door itself was blown back on its hinges by the steep wind, and she pushed her shoulder hard against it until it closed and the room fell silent. She rested her forehead upon the wood a moment, then turned to survey the wreckage of the kitchen. Standing unsteadily on the far side of the room was the kitchen girl, Brigid.

40

That night, after retrieving the she-goat from the girl and the Colonel's sons, he made a supper of a few eggs he had brought home with him from Fells Corner. The chickens were clucking their way toward consensus in their hutch, while nearby the billy and she-goat were tucked cozily into a patch of bracken fern. Bright stood in the doorway of the cabin, looking off toward the ridge as if he could tunnel through it with his eyes and see Rachel once more. His fork scraped against the dish as he ate. When he was done, he walked across his little farmyard and stooped to wash his dish in the stream.

"Henry Bright."

He didn't move.

"Henry Bright," the angel said again. "Henry Bright, I found you. Fear not."

He felt the sigh on the back of his neck and the heat of the angel's nearness, but he gave no answer and continued the washing up as if he were completely alone. When at last it seemed he might rinse the plate forever, he twisted his neck around and looked up into the deep pool of breathing black that was his new horse. "Yeah," he said. "You found me, all right." Then he stood up and, turning his back on the animal, walked across the yard to tether the goats.

"Your time has come, Henry Bright," the horse said behind him. "A great work is demanded of you."

"I don't know you," he said. "You'd better git on out of that horse. That's my horse. If you want a horse, there's a auction over in Fells Corner."

"You know me, Henry Bright. The angel from the church ceiling."

"No, I do not know you. And I don't want to know you either." He walked to the cabin and went in and sat there on the edge of the bed. As evening began to deepen, he came back to the door and stood looking out. "Everybody wants my animals," he said, and threw the flap shut again. A little while later, a metallic clatter arose in the yard. It continued for several minutes and Bright, exasperated, finally threw open the cabin flap to investigate the noise. The horse stood in the middle of the farmyard, looking at him expectantly, one of its back feet standing in the bucket Bright had left at the creek side. He went to the horse and lifted its hoof out of the bucket. "Anyway," he said, "how am I supposed to know it's you?"

"You know it's me."

"How'd you find me?"

"Never mind that. Your great work awaits you."

Bright walked to the doorway of the cabin once more. "I don't want any of your great-work talk. I'm going to work in the coal mines."

"You are not going to work in the coal mines. You are going to marry the girl Rachel and have a son."

"I can't believe you," Bright said.

"You have been chosen, Henry Bright. You will marry her and she will bear your child. She has been chosen to be the mother of the Future King of Heaven."

"You're crazy, angel. You talk like you never heard there was a Jesus Christ before."

"Why do you say that, Henry Bright?"

"Because that's what Jesus Christ is, right? He's the King of Heaven."

"Is he?"

"That's what they say, yeah."

"Yes, they do," the horse said, chewing on the thought. "They do say that, don't they?" There was silence. Then, "What about the barbed wire? Is he King of that? And the mustard gas?"

"How do I know?" Bright stood facing the horse head-on. "You're the angel who was always saying he knew everything."

"Or the shells? The trench mortars? The Spanish flu? Do you remember the flu, Henry Bright? The men drowning of it in the trenches? Is Jesus Christ, the King of Heaven, the King of the Spanish Flu? Of the smells? Of the shit and piss? Is Jesus Christ, the King of Heaven, King of all that misery as well?"

"So what if he is?" Bright said. "I don't care anymore."

"You don't mean that, Henry Bright. Please come to one side so that I might look at you when you address me."

Bright stared deep into one of the horse's eyes, as if he were looking through a hole in the world. "You left me when I got shot. We're finished, you and me."

"Answer me, Henry Bright: Is Jesus Christ the King of everything that you've seen?"

"Maybe he is."

"Why do you suppose a good King would let all those things happen? Doesn't a King have the power to stop them?"

"Why are you making me say all these things? I don't know why he does what he does—"

"Nor do I," the horse said. "Nor do I. The cruelty I've seen is beyond my understanding. So I've decided we need a new King of Heaven."

Bright stood a long moment in the darkness, the empty

177

bucket dangling in his hand. A valedictory stream of urine shot from the horse, drumming hollowly against the ground, as if there were only a thin crust of earth between its hooves and the underworld. Bright peered about him and into the woods, but there was nothing out there. "I don't want to be talking to you anymore," he said finally. "Do you hear me, angel? I didn't ask for you to come around here. You left me out there all shot up and I didn't hear from you for months. Now you're here, just fresh as a strawberry and won't get out of my horse, and talking like you always talked, like nothing ever happened."

"You were never abandoned, Henry Bright. I saved you many times. Remember the graveyard, when the shell landed in front of you and did not explode? And what about in the village? How was it that you kept living while so many others did not? I saved you from drinking the poisoned water and from being discovered as you lay in the ditch. I kept you from being buried along with Sergeant Matthews, and I saved you from being shot in the head on the last day of the War. Who was it but me that grabbed your leg and pulled you to the ground where you would be safe? I saved your life hundreds of times, thousands of times. The bullets that came for you were legion. Tell me truthfully: If not for me, would you have lived?"

"I don't know."

"Yes, you do."

"Well, anyway, I didn't ask you for any of that."

"Of course you did. From the very first moment you heard my voice, you called out to me without ceasing."

"What about all them others? Why was it me you saved and not any of them?"

"Because I chose you, Henry Bright. That day in the church, when you looked up at me, I knew that you alone were the one to help me bring the Future King of Heaven into the world. He is the son you will have with the girl, and, come that great day

178

when the boy takes his throne, men will no longer be forced to kill other men. They will farm, work a trade, marry. They will die in their beds. War will be a thing of the past."

He walked to the creek, dipped the bucket in the water, and set it near the horse for the animal to drink. At the cabin door he lifted the flap, then stood there in the triangle of light for a long moment.

It was four nights later that he saddled the horse and set out toward the Colonel's house to bring back his bride.

41

After Amelia was gone, he held the comb up to the dim light of the window once more. A hairline crack ran grayly up one of the fine white tines. The woman carved into the comb's base looked accusingly at him for this. He held her face up nearer to the window, but the fire had turned the sky the color of engraver's ink, and the only real illumination came from the treetops pluming brightly at the lawn's edge. He pulled her tiny face very close to his own, trying to read her expression, and in doing so the tines seemed to catch a figure running jerkily between them toward the barn. The figure was as thin as a scarecrow, his hat pulled down hard over his pate, his face slanted down against the wind. He wore an outmoded military jacket, and across his back, pulled tight with its tiny burden, hung the sling that Bright had made from Rachel's dress.

42

He threw the door open and stood disoriented in the hallway. It was white plaster and stretched away forever in both directions, the distances measured in potted ferns and musty prints of hunting dogs and prize thoroughbreds. He chose a direction and ran past the numberless doors and flocked wallpaper until he arrived at the brass portals of two elevators. He stood wavering before these, then saw the stairwell beckoning to him through an inconspicuous doorway only a few yards farther on. He threw himself down the steps three and four at a time, holding on to the banisters so that his momentum wouldn't carry him crashing into the plaster busts and knickknacks that crammed the landings. The stairway became more and more crowded with people the closer he got to the ground floor. By the time he rounded the second-floor landing, it felt as if he was wading in a living river of animals, children, nannies, and noise. He pushed his way down into the midst of the confusion and caught a glimpse of the girl Margaret, still directing her brood. He squeezed by her into the domed lobby. Everywhere, trunks and bags were being loaded on large pallets, and porters rushed about, writing on tags and directing one another. Well-dressed men and women stood on the fringes of the activity putting on and taking off gloves, fanning themselves with summer hats, worrying buttons. Children chased one another gleefully through the maze of legs and luggage beneath the dome, climbing on sofas, on hand trolleys, even up on the stately black piano, which stood like a river rock in the middle of the floor.

He wove and jostled his way through the frantic cauldron to the revolving doors and, passing through them, ran down the wide white hotel steps to the drive. Automobiles were backed up fender to fender, adding their own smoke to the air as they vied for space and their drivers shouted at one another. Through the human and mechanical commotion came, at intervals, the velveteen drip of wildlife careening onto the grass from through the gaps in the burning curtains beyond. In the midst of all this, no one seemed to notice Henry Bright as he ran in desperation toward the fire and the barn that it was about to devour.

It looked like the outskirts of the War: carts and horses, huffing engines of all kinds, women and children without homes, and men digging into the dirt to save a piece of ground that only seemed like theirs in that single, desperate moment. The wildfire was a living angry thing in front of him. He could feel the ground itself getting hotter through the soles of his boots, and he was tossed about by gusts of grit-streaked wind. Above its rushing in his ears, he heard another sound and realized that he was screaming, just as he always had when the order came and he fixed his bayonet and climbed up over the sandbags to cross the fields. Then suddenly he was at the lawn's edge, and the world had gotten so atrociously loud and leaden with heat that even the noises coming from his own throat were lost.

Each step toward the incandescent whiteness of the barn became a step into the forge. He skirted a row of rattling cornstalks, moving along the barn's broad side until he came around to the front of the building and could see where its doors hung open. A man's body lay there in the doorway amid a blizzard of white chicken feathers. His neck was a lattice of cuts and scrapes, his dead eyes filled with the same look of insult and terror that crosses an animal's face as it is dragged into the underbrush.

In the midst of the heat, a cold yellow wave of fear sloshed up in Bright's chest. He spun, certain that Corwin and Duncan were behind him, but no one was there. His eyes roved the long row of cornstalks, searching them for faces, but the husks only clapped against each other merrily and gave nothing away. He turned back toward the body lying in the barn doorway and found himself face-to-face with his horse. The animal stood before him, lock-kneed and rigid, its mouth flecked with spittle, its flanks quivering. The black eyes rolled and the big nose snuffed hard against the thick air. The Colonel sat high astride the animal, the baby in the sling upon his chest, the gaping muzzle of the gun pointed down at Bright's head. The horse canted nervously to the left but the Colonel pulled it back to true, hauling viciously on the reins, cutting the bit deep beneath its lolling tongue.

Bright looked up into the black length of the barrel. "That's my mother's rifle."

The old man's eyes glinted. He kicked the horse hard and the animal lunged forward, knocking Bright back against the side of the barn wall with its shoulder. "All your running away," he said, "and you run right to me. A coward always ends up running toward what he wishes to escape. There is no irony in it." He glanced to either side, looking for something. "My goddamn boys are off somewhere," he said. "My useless goddamn boys are off somewhere, but"—he pushed the muzzle of the rifle forward into Bright's face—"it makes no difference to you and me."

Bright looked past the gun into the horse's eyes. "You're gonna let him kill me now?"

"Fear not, Henry Bright." The angel's voice was calm.

183

"But I did everything you told me to!"

"All is well."

Forgetting the rifle pointed down at him, he stepped toward the horse. The Colonel kicked him in the teeth, knocking him painfully back against the barn wall again. His eyes had begun to water hard from the smoke, burning so that it was a struggle to keep them open.

"My daughter." The Colonel, too, was weeping as he ran a sleeve across his mouth. "She was my beautiful girl. You stole her away from me." The tears streamed freely down his face and dropped onto his grandchild as he looked down at the infant. For a moment the old man on the horse seemed to forget that Bright was even there, then his head snapped up once more. "You stole her away from me just like your mother tried to do," he said. "I should have killed you both. I should have shot you down when you were small and buried you where you fell." A thick cloud of smoke enveloped them. The Colonel doubled over, coughing in the saddle. The rifle barrel dipped as he struggled for breath.

"Stay very still, Henry Bright," the angel commanded serenely. "Stay very still and close your eyes."

Another rolling barrage of heat washed over them as the bales of hay inside the barn caught fire. The wind whipped the Colonel's hat off and sucked it behind him into the whirling vortex. He didn't seem to notice. He pulled the rifle hammer back.

Henry Bright looked up into the Colonel's eyes briefly, but the fear was gone, and neither the old man or the waiting infinity of the rifle were of interest anymore. He found that all he wanted to do in the remaining moments of his life was to look at his son. The baby seemed strangely at peace in the conflagration. His coppery hair blew out in all directions. Bright realized that he, too, felt a kind of peace.

If he had lived, it occurred to him, he might have eventually felt that same kind of peacefulness at home, watching his boy grow up. He would have tended to his chickens and rabbits and goats and taught his son the things that his own mother had taught him. And, should he ever again smell the scent of lemons, he might one day have been able to think of sweet tea or lemonade instead of a pile of bodies on the edge of a ragged November tree line.

Maybe, he thought. If he had lived.

He thought about Rachel, whom he had loved since they were small. He felt happy to have held, even for a short while, the son whom she had delivered into his arms. He wondered if his own father had felt such a moment of grace as the earth collapsed around him.

He took one last look at his son and closed his eyes.

The last thing he felt before he heard the gunshot was the breath of the angel on his cheek. After that there was nothing but the heat and the drifting sensation of time continuing to pass in the world beyond his eyelids. He was in hell, he thought. In hell or the War.

He opened his burning eyes to find out which it was.

Above him the Colonel sat erect in the saddle, so still that he could have been posing for his portrait. A purple flower had blossomed beneath his right eye. It bloomed, then wilted and ran down over his cheekbone and into his collar. The old man's face sagged, and then his head drooped and he looked down at his chest as if someone were in the process of pinning a medal there.

The Colonel slumped forward in the saddle. Behind him, a pistol in his outstretched arm, was a man Bright had never seen before. Next to him, faces white and slick with sweat, stood Amelia and Brigid. The Colonel listed in the saddle, his deadweight pulling the horse off balance. Bright pushed away from the barn wall, lunging to catch the old man's body before it toppled off the horse and crushed his son.

The horse began to stamp, but Bright grabbed a stirrup and held the animal where it was as Brigid rushed forward and took the reins. He couldn't reach high enough to pull the sling over the Colonel's head, so he began to ease the body gently down out of the saddle. The buttons of the old man's jacket were hot to the touch.

He saw his mother's rifle only as it slipped from the Colonel's hands. It fell to the ground, firing its single charge. Angel or no angel, the sound of the shot was finally too much for the horse. It went wild, pulling away from Brigid and charging toward Amelia and the man with the pistol as Bright fought hard to hold on. The child bounced crazily in the sling around the dead man's drooping neck.

A second shot sounded, and the rampaging animal, seeming to remember something all of a sudden, went instantly still. It hung there frozen a moment, then collapsed on Henry Bright, pinning him to the ground by his legs. Lawrence reached down and fired a final, merciful shot into its head.

Brigid knelt. "Are you all right?" He answered something, but she was already intent on pulling the infant from the sling.

"You're cracked, H.!" Amelia bent over and yelled down at him. "I tell you to stay put and order room service and this happens?" She watched as Lawrence jammed the Colonel's rifle stock between the horse's hindquarters and the ground. He and Amelia began to lever the deadweight slowly off Bright's legs.

Bright pushed and scraped against the hot ground with his hands and elbows until he'd pulled his feet free and he could stand. They ran from the barn, doubled over, through throes of corrosive soot, washed forward by the percussive *whoosh* of exploding trees, surfacing finally on the great lawn like castaways.

The air was still brutally hot and he struggled to catch his breath as he looked over at Brigid holding his son. She looked back at him, her eyes widening, and yelled something that he couldn't make out. Only when he felt his hair catch fire did he realize that his jacket was burning. He ran to the nearest of the small ponds and threw himself in.

Brigid came to the water too, and he sloshed to the girl's side. She was looking down at the ashen-faced child with deep concern. The boy lay totally still, his expression a mask. Bright reached for the bundle in disbelief, but Brigid slapped his hands away. She bent and dunked the child in the water and, as if reborn, the boy came up howling.

Amelia and Lawrence stood at the pond's edge looking back at the fire. The barn gave way to the flames all at once, as if it had suddenly been transformed into a great swarm of black bees, which at some signal went buzzing heavenward together. Amelia slipped her arm around Lawrence, whom she would marry in the fall, when the weather cooled and the humidity died down. Bright and Brigid looked down at Henry. As she had lifted the infant from the water, the boy had opened his eyes for the first time. They were beautiful and blue, just like Rachel's had been.

They were coming up the bank when the figure of a man staggered out of the fire and stood encased in the dirty-yellow no-man's-land between the trees and the pond as if trapped in amber. Although he made no sound, a serrated cry of alarm came cutting through the roar of the fire from the animal he carried on his back.

By the time Bright reached him, Duncan had sunk to his knees. He tried to pull the goat from his shoulders, but Duncan held the creature's hooves tightly in his fists, unwilling or unable to let go. Bright knocked Duncan to the ground and climbed on top of him, as if he meant to choke him. Duncan made no move either to resist or to let go of the goat, and after a long, tangled moment, Bright grabbed the Colonel's son by his hair and shirtfront and pulled him to his feet. He shoved him, the goat still on his back, to the pond's edge and pushed Duncan in. As he hit the water, the goat finally kicked herself free of Duncan's grip and stood shakily sneezing in the mud.

"I found her," Duncan said, sitting up in the water. "She was running around in the fire and I caught her." He leaned forward and took a drink of water. "Do you have the baby?" Soaked, Duncan looked more like a child than a man. "He's my sister's baby."

"Yes," Bright said. "Come on." The goat was looking at him across the water, as if trying to remember something. A dream came back to him then. In it he was kicking Duncan in the head.

Duncan woozily reached around in the pond for the goat. It made no struggle as he scooped it into his arms again. "I think I need help walking," he said.

"Where did you come from?" He helped the Colonel's son up the bank.

"Corwin and me weren't allowed to stay inside the hotel with the other folks 'cause of some of the things he used to do. They all blamed me too. One of them knocked me down and he was beating me, but a man from the hotel stopped him. We still had to leave, though, so we went to the barn." Duncan coughed. His ribs seemed about to poke through his skin. "And at the barn there was all these chickens. I looked at Corwin. I saw what was in his mind."

Bright looked in those deep-set eyes. "Where's Corwin?"

"That hotel man came across the field just when Corwin was starting in on the chickens. He tried to stop Corwin but it wasn't no use. He didn't know about my brother. Corwin knocked him down and then . . . He wouldn't stop. Finally I took a shovel and I hit Corwin over the head with it real hard and it killed

188

him. That didn't make no difference to the hotel man, though. He was already gone. I saw my father coming across the field, so I dragged my brother over behind the barn. Your goat was standing there. She took one little look at me and just lit out. I said to myself, 'She's gonna run right into the fire.' So I chased after her until I caught her."

He looked around wildly. "Where's he at? My father?"

"He died," Bright said. "I'm sorry," he added.

"I'm not."

They passed a group of men going in the opposite direction, shepherding the big pumper toward the pond. Some were already wearing gas masks. Farther on, others were just setting out for the fire, most still dressed raggedly in the clothes that they had been wearing when they were driven from their homes. Among them were some of the hotel guests in shirtsleeves, their faces blanching in the temperature. Near the gate, people worked furiously to dig firebreaks with whatever they had. Some used shovels, but others turned the ground with hoes, knives, even spoons. The auntly woman from the general merchandise store was there, ripping great, green chunks of soil and grass from the ground with a pickax. A line of children waited with buckets at a water pump by the kitchen entrance. A hose now ran out of the fountain and was being used to wet the lawn.

"Kill him, Henry Bright."

Bright heard the voice but did not stop walking.

"Henry Bright, you must kill Duncan. Then we will find a mother for the child." Bright glanced toward the goat hanging exhausted in Duncan's arms. Even its ears dangled listlessly. Suddenly it looked up at him, its pupils golden keyholes, its voice serene and confident. "He must die, Henry Bright. The safety of the Future King of Heaven demands it."

Bright looked away and didn't speak. They rejoined Brigid

189

and his boy in the milling crowd near the fountain. The girl held the child closely and smiled as Bright approached. He reached out and touched his son's hair. "I have to do something," he told her. "I'll be back directly."

He turned to Duncan. "I was in the War. I went to France and I saw some things there." He paused. "No, I saw a lot of things that I wish I'd never seen. Awful things. Sometimes I still see them." Bright's hands clenched tightly at his sides, and he ground his teeth as he fought with some inner thought. Then, suddenly, "Were you there?"

"Where?" Duncan asked.

"Did you go to the War? Did you come out of the farmhouse that night?"

For once, the black stones of Duncan's eyes seemed to register surprise. "Me?" he said. "I never been this far from home."

Bright searched those eyes for any traces of the farmhouse that might be hidden in them. Then his face relaxed and the tautness went out of his shoulders. He reached out to pet the goat in Duncan's arms. "I guess you were right about one thing after all," he said to it.

"What?" Duncan asked.

"I have to take my goat now," Bright said to him. "Don't you worry, she'll be safe. Maybe you and I will find a new goat when this is all over," he added.

Duncan gave the goat to Bright and sat down on the edge of the fountain.

"You must kill him, Henry Bright. If you do, I will help you find a mother for your son."

At his feet, the hotel steps rippled upward like the train of a wedding dress. He ascended them, the she-goat tucked under his arm, and passed through the revolving doors into the silence of the now-deserted lobby. Once inside, man and goat looked up into that domed sweep of beneficent blue sky, so different from the apocalyptic orange world without.

At the center of the great, round room, beneath the eternal early-fall clarity of the painted dome, stood the batholithic piano, impenetrably dark. He carried the creature across the room toward the glossy black slab, turning a slow full circle and checking that the sky above them was as empty as it had appeared earlier. When he was sure that it was, he placed the she-goat atop the piano. Her hooves clicked soundingly against the ebony, causing faint vibrations in the strings. Somehow the sounds were magnified beneath the high ceiling, as if, high above, a discordant orchestra had begun to tune.

"Jee-roosh needs a mother, Henry Bright. The Future King of Heaven needs someone to care for him until he can take the throne."

"Enough of that," Bright said. "Keep it. I've heard enough."

"Do as I say!"

"We've had our differences, you and me, but everyone should have a home, and it weren't a trouble to bring you here. You kept me safe when I was in the War, and maybe I wouldn't have married Rachel if it wasn't for you, and maybe we wouldn't a had a son." He paused to consider the thought. "Maybe that's all true. I don't have any idea one way or the other. But I do know that without you, I wouldn't have burned down our cabin and the whole forest and all those people's homes and let my horse get shot. And," he said, "I wouldn't have let anybody make me believe I couldn't raise my own boy."

He looked at the goat. "I hope that this place will make you happy. If the fire don't reach the hotel I guess you'll be safe enough. There's no one else around you in that sky to bother you, so just get out of that goat and go on up there now. Git."

"Don't leave me here, Henry Bright," the angel commanded.

191

"Maybe if you're happy here," Bright continued, "you'll just let me go on about my life with my boy." He looked up into the blue and closed his eyes a moment. He was very tired.

"I know you're angry with me," he said, opening them again after a while. The goat was staring at him ponderously, her little teeth sliding back and forth against one another. He smiled at this. "I guess that's all a load of junk you told me about the King of Heaven and everything, but if any of it is the truth, if my son Henry really is the future King of Heaven, then I figure when he gets old enough, if you're still mad at me for leaving you here, maybe he can straighten things out between the two of us."

He leaned over the piano's edge and kissed the goat on her nose. The animal snuffled at the collar of his uniform, and the two of them stayed there a long moment. Then, without looking back, Bright spun on his heels and strode out from beneath the cool light of the dome and through the revolving doors.

At the edge of the lawn, the tumult of flames and smoke was smearing the sky into the ground. Toward the fire's sway marched lines of men and women, holding tiny buckets of water with which to soak the grass. At times throughout the night, they seemed to turn from real, living people into mere photographs of people, and then from photographs into memories, which are like photographs, and finally, as the ground blurred beneath them, whatever parts of them that could be seen from afar seemed to float like ghosts in the rippling air as they went about their work.

He descended the steps and wove his way back through the crowd of refugees. Amelia and Lawrence, arm in arm, were being fretted over by a knot of well-dressed people. Duncan stood near them, looking about him at the world through red-rimmed eyes as if for the first time. Bright found Brigid where he had left her, holding his son in her arms. He smiled at her and she returned the smile. He looked into his son's blue eyes and laughed. It was a strange sound to hear coming from his mouth. He leaned forward to kiss the boy's forehead. With her free hand, Brigid reached out and brushed stiff, white goat hairs from the shoulders of his jacket and then gently pulled him forward by a lapel and kissed his own smoke-stained forehead. He looked at the mother and child together for a long time and then made to join some men heading to fight the fire. Abruptly, though, he turned to face her once more and, drawing from his pocket a small and ancient ivory comb, he pressed it into her hand for safekeeping.

Acknowledgments

This book would not have been possible without my editor, Noah Eaker. Great thanks as well to Scott Moyers. Thanks to my manager and friend, Darius Zelkha, and to Tim Craven, Liam Hurley, Austin Nevins, Sam Kassirer, Zack Hickman, the Ricks, the Leahys, Mary Moyer, Carla Sacks, Maria Braeckel, Kathy Lord, Dave Brewster, Sue Devine, Doug Rice, Dave O'Grady, Dan Cardinal, Brian Stowell, Scott Hueston, Robert Pinsky, Ed Romanoff, Jonathan Horn, and Kathleen Denney.

Much respect is due to Barbara Tuchman for her books *The Proud Tower* and *The Guns of August;* Joseph Persico for his *Eleventh Month, Eleventh Day, Eleventh Hour;* and to William Orpen's *An Onlooker in France, 1917–1919.* These books are requiems.

Most especially, thank you to my family—Robert, Sue, Lincoln, and Chana—the best of the better angels.

About the Author

JOSH RITTER is a songwriter from Moscow, Idaho. His albums include *The Animal Years* and *So Runs the World Away*. *Bright's Passage* is his first novel. He currently lives in New York.

www.joshritter.com

About the Type

This book was set in Baskerville, a typeface which was designed by John Baskerville, an amateur printer and type-founder, and cut for him by John Handy in 1750. The type became popular again when The Lanston Monotype Corporation of London revived the classic Roman face in 1923. The Mergenthaler Linotype Company in England and the United States cut a version of Baskerville in 1931, making it one of the most widely used typefaces today.